Other Stories & Rosie Wreay

Story Times 3

Brindley Hallam Dennis

Copyright © 2016 Brindley Hallam Dennis

All rights reserved.

ISBN:1539046567
ISBN-13:9781539046561

DEDICATION

To all readers of short stories
And especially those of mine

CONTENTS

	Acknowledgments	i
1	Final Accounts	1
2	Men	26
3	Situations	49
4	Mildred's Recollections	104
5	Eight Frames for Rosie Wreay	122
6	Anomalies	142

ACKNOWLEDGMENTS

Final Accounts is available as a download from CUTalongstory.
Dawn Chorus was longlisted in a Flash500 competition.
Henry & Mr Oufle, *First Foot* & *The Hotel Entrance* have been performed by Liars league in Hong Kong and London and can be found on their websites.
Woy Dincha? first appeared in the Black Market Review.
Hanley was first published in .Cent magazine.
Seemingley By Accident was included in the Flash Flood Journal.
The Silence was Highly Commended in a HISSAC competition.
The Best He Could Do won 2nd prize in a TSS Flash Fiction competition.

1 FINAL ACCOUNTS
(TEN FLASH FICTIONS)

Timing

James hobbled to the front door. Rosie was hanging on the bell, probably assuming he couldn't hear it. He'd seen her from the upstairs window, but it took him longer to get down these days.

Hello Rosie.

Hi Jim. Forty years, he thought, and she still hasn't picked up on it. It was his fault. He should have corrected her that first time.

And this is James and Elaine. I work with James sometimes.

Hi Jim.

Too late now, he thought, and he remembered the way that frown used to unroll itself across Frank's forehead every time. Poor Frank. Poor Ellie.

Well, are you going to let me in?

Sorry, yes. He pivoted backwards on his good leg, moved

sideways like a ruined crab. Go through to the kitchen.

Rosie was still slim. Cadaverous in fact. She always had been. Skeletal. Brittle. Her hair was still good – henna red – and she wore bright red lipstick; but she dressed like a man. James had always thought that if she had dressed differently she would have been a different woman; but then, she would have needed to be a different woman to dress differently. He followed her down the hall. She had a boney arse, he thought. It would be like banging a folded deck-chair. He should have screwed her though, that time he had the chance. It would have done her good. Too late now. She'd never be able to get it up, and besides, he no longer needed to be unfaithful to Ellie.

You blew it Rosie, he said out loud without meaning to.

What?

Sorry?

She thought better of it and pulled a chair out from under the kitchen table. She sat down and spoke as if in answer.

A coffee would be nice.

Coffee it is then. He could get it up, he reminded himself, remembering Ellie, but he had no desire to connect with anyone else these days, not really. Legs were nice though, but not in jeans. He remembered the old joke: not fat ones, not thin ones, but something in between. He laughed, turning to the cupboards to reach down mugs.

So. Are you OK? Rosie asked, putting a concerned look on her face.

I'm fine, he said. And you? That was a mistake, he thought. He braced himself for the usual onslaught. He had the time though, and wasn't that what friends were for? Rosie said nothing. He looked around.

I guess so, she said. That sounded serious. He made the coffees and swung around to the table on his good leg.

You don't sugar.

No.

You don't milk.

No.

That's what I thought. He set the mugs down and Rosie reached out and slowly, with her finger, by the handle, turned it around, like an exhibit on a lazy susan. She had that soft look in her eye that had always made him think she needed a good screw. This was only the second time she had let that look show when they were alone.

It's not as if we were still, she paused, and he wondered what particular word she was searching for. Accounted for, she finished. His face was a question mark. You know, she said, married.

You've lost me. She reversed the turning mug, avoiding his eyes.

We can have sex with whoever we like. His mouth fell slightly open and he hastily lifted his own mug and took a sip. The coffee was too hot, and tasteless. It's not such a big thing, she went on, to do it for a friend.

I suppose not, he said, wondering who the doer might be, and who the done for.

Frank and I, she began. He did not want to hear this. He and Ellie, of course, had talked about them. That was natural. How else did you work out where your own sex-life fitted into the spectrum of normality? They'd always thought that Frank and Rosie both needed a good fucking. He'd thought it of Rosie, and there had been that one time when they had nearly; when he had nearly. Ellie had thought it of Frank. Neither of them, so far as he knew, had done anything about it. Rosie was looking at him. He wondered what she was expecting him to say. Well, she prompted. Do you want to?

Did she want him to fuck her? Or was she offering to fuck him? She was twenty years too late. Forty, he corrected himself. No, fifty. The years kept on rolling. A laugh built up inside him and he froze it to a grin. He would have fucked anything in a skirt once. But she was right. They could fuck whoever the hell they wanted to now. They were beyond all those artificial constraints. They were free. It was a revelation. But he had no desire for her. And that charity thing – not such a big thing to do for a friend. He didn't like that whichever end of it you were going to be on. He didn't want to be rude, to insult or disappoint her.

He remembered Frank, decades ago, confessing to an infidelity, before Rosie's time. He had confessed to his girlfriend too, had said those exact words. I didn't want to disappoint her, and the girlfriend had told him, I admire your generosity, before throwing him out.

Nice thought, Rosie, James said. He wondered what to say, and then thought of his medication. The trouble is, since I've been on the tablets, I don't even get to think about it. It would be like getting the toothpaste back in the tube. He laughed and raised his arms. See, I'm helpless, they said. He could see she was surprised.

I'm sorry, she said. I didn't realise. She was, too. He could see that, and all the affection he had for her flowed out like thawed ice. He reached across and touched her hand.

I've always been really fond of you, he said, his eyes filling up.

Me too, she said.

And it was true; and they could have behaved quite differently, in the past, in the present.

After she'd gone he phoned Mary.

Hello James, do you want the old bugger?

Is he in?

He's asleep in the conservatory. Shall I wake him?

No. It's you I want to talk to.

Final Accounts

Wilson didn't know he had only one week to live, whereas Seymour had been warned that he would die within the year. He was already too ill to drive, so he asked Wilson to take him to see her.

Wilson was reluctant, but they had been friends for decades.

Take a week's leave, Seymour said.

Wilson's wife, knew the value of friendship, and she told him to get on with it. You never knew what they meant by 'within the year'. Why, it might happen the next week, who could tell? Wilson knew how important it was to Seymour that he got to see her one more time, but he was uncomfortable about Seymour's wife.

What'll you tell her? He asked.

We don't have to tell her anything, Seymour said, except that we're going away. But Wilson worried that he'd have to maintain the deception for the rest of his life. I need to speak to her, Seymour said, face to face.

Wilson knew what had happened last time she and Seymour had met face to face, or at least he guessed. What was worse, Wilson would have to make the arrangements. Seymour hadn't been in touch with her for years, he said. His wife had made him promise. He didn't even have an address or phone number, written down. They weren't connected on social media or by e-mail, apparently. Wilson had kept in touch though, for old time's sake. It would be the last time, Wilson thought, that he would have to do something like this for his friend, which was true.

They stayed at a country pub not far from where she lived, taking a twin bedded room. Wilson stayed down in the bar while they talked upstairs. He expected they'd both come down for a last drink together before she left. Unless, that was, she took Seymour off with her, Wilson thought.

But earlier than expected she came down alone, crossed the bar without speaking or even looking towards Wilson, and left. He saw her though. Her face was red and puffy, as if she had been crying. Seymour didn't appear, and when Wilson went up he found him sitting on the bed, his face as pale as the ceiling and the tracks of tears marking his chin. He looked worse than Wilson had ever seen him.

She said she hated me, Seymour said. She said I'd wasted her life; that I was already dead as far as she was concerned. Seymour looked like a broken man and Wilson was afraid that he wouldn't make it through the night, but it was Wilson who had the heart attack. Seymour told me the story decades later, following what the doctors called his miraculous remission.

Leaving It So Late

When he rang it was already late.

Pete had started to get ready for bed. She thought immediately that no-one would ring at that time of night unless it were an emergency.

Do you want me to get it? Pete shouted down.

I'll go! She picked up the kitchen phone. Hello?

Jill.

Mark! She felt for a chair and sat down.

I need to see you.

All the questions tumbled through her mind. Where? When? Why? What the hell are you doing ringing this late? When was it she had last heard his voice, except in her head?

I'm coming over.

What?

I'll be there in about five hours.

You're still at home? It would take at least that long. The phone went dead. Mark? Mark!

Everything all right? Pete's voice made her jump. He'd come downstairs. Who was it? She could see from his face that he'd heard. She sought for an answer, but only silence came. I see.

Would you mind. She could feel herself blushing, not staying tonight?

If that's what you want.

I'm sorry.

He turned away. She shouldn't do this. Mark shouldn't do it, not after all these years. She shouldn't need to. She looked at the clock. Half eleven. It would be nearly light by the time he arrived. Pete had vanished back upstairs. She could hear him moving about, packing his bag. She glanced around the kitchen. She had never encouraged him to leave his stuff. Why was that?

An unbidden lightness bubbled up within her, a delight. She wanted to laugh out loud.

Because she had always hoped for this call. She had always expected it. Pete was coming down the stairs. They passed awkwardly in the narrow kitchen.

I'll..

He shook his head and went outside. She bit her lip; waited until she heard the sound of his car. She had never made any promises. He had never asked her to. Then she turned and went upstairs. She needed to change the sheets.

She was asleep in the chair, and woke to the sound of a car door, and the glow of the outside light, faintly brighter than the grey pre-dawn. She opened the back door.

Mark had aged. He looked tired, from the long drive. His eyes were dark and heavy. Long grooves, which she had not seen before, lined his cheeks. His throat was a sunken shadow between two taut sinews. But his mouth, his mouth was as it had always been, and she watched it, waiting for him to speak.

Will you look after me? he said. I'm dying.

Maisie Seddon's Lover

The pub, just across the village green, had laid on quite a spread: open sandwiches, tiers of cakes, scones, tea breads, tray bakes, his favourite chocolate fancies, endless cups of coffee and tea. And for those wanting something alcoholic, the bar was open. There was a real coal fire, chuckling like a mountain stream, and most of the mourners, or should one think of them as guests, had flowed towards that end of the room. The lamps had been lit, though it could only have been a little after three, but the day was already grey. It was damp, and grey and nearly over. Deep pools of shadow had seeped into the room from the corners and from between the low timbers of the ceiling.

Martin had headed for the bar, after he'd finished his self-appointed task of officiating at the door, thanking everyone for coming, and taking their offered hands in both of his, exchanging smoothly polished platitudes, as if he were the bloody vicar. She had allowed herself to be manoeuvred into a corner, where she was not exactly sidelined, but wasn't in a pole position either, so to speak. She wasn't a widow, when all was said and done. Now Martin was approaching her with a glass of red wine his hand. One glass, she noticed. Mind you, she'd already looked after herself in that respect, as you would have expected. She watched his approach through steady grey eyes that were not in the least red-rimmed. She had done her crying in private, and any more that needed to be done she would do in the same milieu.

Well, Martin said, and then he waggled his head slightly like an angler twitching a hooked worm. She said nothing but continued to stare. It makes you quite someone, he said at last.

It?

Being his last lover. He smiled, then sipped from the wine.

And you, she replied, being his oldest friend.

That's not the same.

No. Briefly she turned up the corner of her mouth. But someone, she said, nevertheless.

Four years wasn't it?

Since?

That you were...He let the sentence drift downstream, the words, fucking him, floating through his mind. Since you became an item. He and Martin had been friends for over forty.

Thereabouts, she admitted. She let her gaze slip off over his shoulder to where French windows were closed against a view of the ill-kept garden, already dying back. It was our work that brought us together, she said as if to herself. Martin and he had tried, she knew, decades before, to collaborate, but it had come to nothing. It was my work he really loved.

Martin flushed and took another drink. Her eyes, ignoring him, were beautiful, he had to admit.

Didn't it ever bother you, he said, drawing them back to his face, that you were the spitting image of Maisie Seddon?

Who?

Grain

People had put flowers by the tree. Miller's blood boiled.

He was on his fucking mobile, he said. Sansom shrugged and pulled a face.

We all do it.

I don't fucking do it! Sansom didn't know why Miller was so upset. He wasn't a friend of the family, though they were neighbours. Miller stretched out an open hand. He'd passed me only a couple of days before, in the lane. He was on his mobile then, and he waved to me. With his other fucking hand.

Those tractors have power steering, Sansom said. They're solid as a rock. He shook his head and made as if to walk on, but Miller was rooted to the ground, looking down at the bunches of flowers.

She was in the cab then too, he said, the little girl.

I suppose he'd done it a hundred times before.

Oh, and that makes it OK? You could see she wasn't strapped in.

You never know what's coming round the bend, Sansom said, and he glanced along the road to where it curved away ahead between hedges. Miller stared at him with raised eyebrows. Yes, I know, Sansom said. He shrugged again, lifting his own hands in a gesture of supplication. The guy must be feeling awful.

It's not all about him though, is it? However he feels, it's not all about him. Miller lowered his head again, but his eyes, from under shadowed brows were on Sansom. He said, I waved back.

Eulogies

When Pooley died, Rustus suggested that everyone in the writing group wrote something on a page torn from one of the Moleskine notebooks he loved so much, and dropped it in the grave. It would be more fitting, he said, than a handful of soil.

Pooley had started the group years before. Rustus had been the only other male, and spare, member. Pooley had flirted with all the others, always, and they had flirted with him.

At the funeral pages fluttered down like confetti, but Rustus held back. Afterwards he returned to the graveside where a weather-beaten labourer was filling in the grave. The man looked up as Rustus approached, and thrust his spade deep into a mound of earth where it quivered slightly. He pulled a wad of clay-stained papers out of his jacket and handed them over. Rustus passed him a plump, clean, white envelope, which the gravedigger pocketed with a grin.

Back in his car, Rustus thumbed through the papers. They were all blank. He turned them over, checking both sides. No-one had written anything, except on the one the gravedigger had put at the bottom of the pile. Rustus swore and crushed the page in his fist.

Always Meant To Be

Pete and me have been mates for years. The last time I saw him he asked me about Jean.

He hadn't mentioned her for years. I thought he'd forgotten all about her. That's why I'd stopped mentioning her. I suppose I'd got a bit fed up with it, in the days when he did want to talk. I mean, it would be every time I saw him. I didn't mind keeping him up to date. I knew they weren't in touch since his marriage.

That was OK for the first couple of years, but when it got past the five year mark it began to irritate. I began to wonder if that was the reason he still did things with me. The worst was when he'd try to slip it in during the conversation without me noticing; as if it were an afterthought, as if it would have been impolite not to. Eventually he began to leave it until the last moment, blurting something out just before we parted. Heard anything of Jean lately? How's Jean doing these days?

It got so that I was waiting for it. Once or twice, when we took trips away, I spent the whole time wondering when he'd hit me with it. When he finally did stop, I couldn't believe it. It was a couple of years before I stopped wondering when she was going to crop up again.

Now, ten years since she had, and with his wife just gone, he'd suddenly asked, is Jean still at the same address? It wasn't just that I thought he'd forgotten about her. Even Sally and I didn't mention her any more. Well, not very often.

We were never friends, he said, on Facebook or anything like that. I deleted her from my address book years ago. He glanced at me. Because of his wife, he meant. I've tried searching for her online, he said, but...He must have seen the surprise in my face. You are still in touch?

    Well, as it happens, I started to say.

    It never occurred to me, he said, that we four would ever lose touch. He meant me and Sally, and him and Jean.

    You haven't mentioned Jean for years, I said. I thought you'd forgotten her.

    No, he said. But I could see it pissed you off that I kept on asking about her.

    I was going to explain, but he carried on. I don't blame you, he said, but things are different now. I'm a free man, and we were always meant to be together. I always knew that, he said.

    It must have showed in my face, because he fell silent and stared at me.

    Pete, I said. Jean died several years ago.

Grave Goods

I'd gone with Patterson to put flowers on his mother's grave. We strolled back towards the lych-gate. Patterson was quiet, and I saw no reason to intrude upon his thoughts. Then he stopped opposite a tombstone and pointed. It was a modern stone, carved in austere lettering, giving only names and dates and, in capitals, RIP. That was my uncle, on my father's side, he said. I smiled, uncertain of how to react. I was with him, he said, on the day he died. I tilted my head in sympathy, and enquiry. An accident, he said, out in the fields.

We stood at the foot of the grave, looking towards the headstone as if at the foot of an invalid's bed.

He was on his back, and bleeding. Dad was with us. He said, keep him calm. The calmer he is, the slower the heart will pump. I must have looked perplexed, for he went on to explain that if you lowered the heart rate, you would lower the rate of blood loss. Dad had his mobile and was trying to phone for help, but the signal was weak. He went off up the hill to try and get a better one, and left me with Uncle Bill. I didn't know what to do at first. I was holding a handkerchief against the wound, but it was already soaked through. Then I thought, get him to talk about something, so I asked him to tell me about the best day of his life.

He looked up at me as if I were mad. He was in pain, I suppose, and frightened. Then his eyes cleared, and he smiled, and he started to tell me about his wedding day. It did the job. It calmed him down. The blood stopped flowing so quickly. It had been coming in spurts before, in time with the heart I guess, but now it was just oozing.

He told me about how beautiful she had looked, his bride; how the birds had sung. It had been a May wedding, and all the flowers were out, He could remember the church bells ringing. Then Dad came back and said they were sending the Air Ambulance, because we were so far from a road. But it was too late. He never made it to the hospital. There were complications, with his heart.

Patterson stared down at the headstone. I didn't know what to say, so I settled for some trite platitude. What other sort is there? That wasn't it, he said. It was when I was talking to my auntie, later. I thought it would cheer her up, if I told her what his last words to me had been. But it didn't. She got really upset.

It was bound to make her sad, I offered, however touching the sentiment.

No, Patterson said, not sad upset. She was livid. Dad told me, later, Uncle Bill got married in December, and in a Registry Office, the second time.

Passing By

A line of young pine trees, mixed with ornamental shrubs, all in flower now that the good weather had finally broken through, edged the garden, save for where the paved terrace overlooked the sea. Here a low wall, built of the flat-slabbed local stone allowed them to look out towards Scotland. Above their heads the breeze off the sea rippled the canvas of the patio canopy.

You could want more than this, Brandt said, counting his blessings, need it even, but if you do, it probably means you'll never be entirely happy with whatever you get. Scotland looked amazingly clear. I've never seen it look so clear, he said.

It was even clearer earlier on, Mark said. He twisted awkwardly in his chair, for he was sitting with his back to the view. The slightest veil of mist hovered, seeming to lie back off the actual coast, covering the rising slopes of Criffel, but this was an illusion for it was in reality quite high above the water surface, so that they were looking through a sort of letter box of clear air. The bright white towers of the wind-farm off the coast sparkled with the sun on them. It's always changing, Mark observed, wincing as he turned back to the table.

Darley was reminiscing about his years in London. He'd worked in advertising. Copy, he was saying, was about telling people what they wanted, in those days.

It still is, isn't it? Mark asked.

No, no. It's more subtle than that now. Darley liked

talking about the old days, but he was glad to be out of it. Nowadays, he said, we tell them about the experience the product will give them. He nodded encouragingly, wanting someone to jump ahead, but no-one did. That way, he explained, they think they are making the decision for themselves. He wished he could think of an example, but he couldn't, and he had forgotten just about every slogan he had ever come up with, though one or two had won prizes, within the industry.

  Brandt smiled and sipped at his by now rather flat fizzy-wine. They did this almost every Sunday, at least when the weather was good: came over to Mark and Marge's place. It was difficult for Mark to get out now, and fraught for both of them if he did. Brandt and Joan, Darley and Sarah, a couple of others were on the list. They were happy to come. There was no way of knowing how much longer they could go on doing it: how many more summers Mark would get; how many more Sundays.

  Sometimes it was just drinks, coffee and cakes, fizzy wine and flap-jack. Sometimes it morphed into lunch. Marge always had something ready. It was all a matter of how Mark was that day. Sometimes it would fall through at the last moment. Then they would get something out of the freezer at home, or go to one of the local pubs, if they could get in at short notice. Long-term planning had gone out of the door where Mark and Marge were concerned. Life was a bitch, Brandt thought, especially if you were in Mark's position. He took the view that they should go whenever they were invited. Your friends need you when they need you, he told Joan, not when it suits you.

Darley and Sarah took the same tack. It's not all about us, they told each other. There would be more weekends to remember, they reminded themselves, if they did it this way; more good times to look back on, after Mark had gone.

We never sat out once last year, Sarah said. Not once!

We had supper outside twice last week, Joan said.

We've stopped having lunch on the terrace, Brandt said. It's too hot!

I can stand any amount of this, Darley said. He was sitting a little way back from the table so that the sun bore down on his uncovered head and shoulders.

You should be more careful, Mark warned him.

I love it, Darley said, the heat. Bring it on.

The sun poured down like hot fat.

Shall we open another bottle of cava? Marge offered. Brandt waved a refusal.

I'm driving.

I can drive, Joan said. I don't want any more anyway.

We can walk home, Darley said. Mark nodded, and Marge got up to go for it.

I'll help, Darley said, and he pushed himself to his feet. He swayed for a moment, looking surprised.

Stood up too quickly, Joan said, reaching towards him, but the surprised look had fixed itself like a clawed hand to Darley's face and he took a pace backwards, swinging around from the table. His chair fell over and he, not even throwing out a hand to save himself, toppled forward onto the brick patio. As he fell a jumble of incomprehensible words came from his mouth.

They organised a wheelchair for Mark, for the funeral, but he was on form that day, and walked slowly the curved path through the graveyard with Brandt at his side. Marge and Joan walked with Sarah. Brandt and Mark glanced at each other from time to time. They both had something to say, about the futility of expectations; about assumptions of who would go first. Brandt had survived chemo-therapy a decade or so back and had seen off a dozen who had wished him well at the time, and thought themselves lucky.

    Are you coming over for lunch on Sunday? Mark asked.

    I hope so!

    We'll see what the weather does.

    Will Sarah come do you think?

    I think she's staying with her daughter for a week or two.

    Brandt nodded.

    We could sit in the conservatory, if it rains, Mark said.

    They got to the graveside and looked in. The coffin was already there, a green cloth softening the exposed edges of the cut. Mark remembered a joke he'd heard, about a piper who was supposed to play at an interment, but who arrived late and mistaking them for grave-diggers, played for two workmen who were burying a new sewage pipe,. He suppressed a laugh and hoped he'd be able to recall it during the sandwiches afterwards. Old pine trees, clothed in sombre green edged the cemetery like ranks of paid mourners waiting their turn, save for a gap where the wrought iron gate stood open to the view of a distant hillside upon which a soft grey cloud of mist lightly rested.

Sometimes Brandt thought about the future; about how soon it would arrive and whose future it would be, but at the graveside he could only think about how smooth the legs of the women looked in their black tights, or were they stockings? And he wished that the breeze, which always seems to blow across graveyards at interments, would lift the hems of their skirts a little higher.

Flying Out

The airport taxi was on its way. The suitcases were packed and waiting in the hall, when the call came through.

Bob could tell it was bad news from the way his wife carried the phone to the bottom of the stairs and sat on the last step. He wondered if it was her mother, or if something had happened to Marcus, but then she covered the mouthpiece and he lip-read the name of Sylvia's husband. There was no other reason for him to call. Sylvia had been in hospital for weeks. Her husband had put on a brave face. Bob and his wife hadn't discussed it explicitly but their conversations had been on the tacit understanding that Sylvia wouldn't be going home. Bob's wife wasn't saying much, but she looked up and drew one extended finger across her throat. Inappropriately comic, but just what Sylvia herself would have done.

The knowledge of her death would be like an invisible extra suitcase that they would take on holiday. They would unpack it along with the others when they reached the resort. The memories of all that the four of them had done together would be inside. They would rummage through them: places they had visited, meals they had taken, conversations they had shared. They would carry some of it down to the beach, take some into the hotel bar. Some they would have as they prepared to sleep. Some they would share over breakfast. Like a long and worthy book, packed to read by the pool, they would work their way through their memories of

Sylvia's life: her successes and failures; her achievements; her unfulfilled ambitions; her missed opportunities. They would talk too about how Sylvia's husband would cope; about the extent to which he had really believed that she would make a full recovery. They would question what they could do to help; to keep him a part of the world.

Bob moved without thinking, across the hall and into the dining room, where he halted by the narrow window that opened out upon the garden, which was a blur of greens and other colours. A noise like rustling paper and a fluttering called to him. A butterfly, dark orange with black markings, had risen from the sill and was throwing itself against the window-pane. He reached out and loosed the catch and pushed the window wide. A sweet honeyed fragrance wafted in from the purple spires of the buddleia that lifted in graceful curves beyond the glass. The butterfly, released from the narrow confines of the room, flew out, upwards, into the clear blue summer sky.

2 MEN
(TEN FLASH FICTIONS)

Stirks

All morning the stirk had stood with its head in the hedge. I could see its black and white rump, a pair of gangly legs and the fly whisk tail. Then it came closer and for a while stood motionless behind a clump of buddleia long past flowering. I could sense it watching me through the arching fronds as I moved about the garden. It seemed unnaturally still.

The back-story was that the field gate had been left open twice in the previous few days, and four stirks had got out into the lane. Then somebody towing a caravan had driven them down before him until they spilled out onto the main road. Three of them had been rounded up and returned to the field, but the fourth had vanished entirely. That was Monday.

This was Thursday. By the time the farmer and his three boys turned up, the one on the quad bike not wearing a helmet – nothing in there worth protecting, pal – the stirk had slumped against the hedgerow, lying awkwardly, as if struck by a vehicle. The tall, thin boy approached and leaned in close.

I heard the word pneumonia spoken, but nothing else was said. The farmer, who must have been my age or even older, glanced at me. It wasn't my garden. I just worked there. I didn't know any of them by name, but had wandered up the drive to see if I could help.

The stirk jumped up when the thin boy grabbed it by the tail and pulled him round behind the buddleia and onto the flower bed, which was raised up and held by a low wall. He let go of the tail and fell, bringing down a couple of the retaining stones.

The jump down brought the stirk to its knees too, and I thought for a moment it must have broken a leg, and would roll onto its side and collapse. But it rose again quickly and clumsily.

Then the stirk rounded on us and stamped its spindly legs, and I realised that this was no rescue by old and trusted friends. Stirks are no good to anyone and are sold off for meat after a short time. Nobody gets to know them well, or to call them by name. They remain strangers, captured by strangers who mean to have them killed.

Then the stirk turned away and trotted back, brisk as a Camargue Bull, towards the lane and the boy on the quad bike raced away ahead of it, presumably to get to the field gate, and the stirk trotted after him.

Then the boy who had fallen, gangly and awkward, and with the same uncomprehending brown eyes, trotted past me too, seemingly unhurt.

I knelt down and pulled the fallen stones away from the wall and cleared out the loose soil and roots that had accumulated there and I put the stones back into place, as securely, and perhaps more so than they had been before.

Krauts

On a village walk I fell in with an old man I'd not met before who pointed out to me the ruins of an old tithe barn. Then, a field further on he started talking about the war, when he had been a boy.

I recalled labourers with German caps, working on the building sites in the nineteen fifties.

He said, German prisoners of war used to work here. Fifty of them, came in on two trucks, with four guards. He said, they had push bikes painted black and white, and he made segments of black and white with his hands along an imaginary cross bar.

We borrowed two of them one day, me and a friend, he said; pedalled off to the coast to look at the aircraft on the airfield. It was a hot day and after we'd stood looking through the perimeter wire for a while, we pushed the bikes down between the dunes, and stripped off and went onto the beach.

Weren't the beaches sealed off, for invasion? I asked.

Down south, mebbe, not up here. We bundled up our clothes and pushed them under a gorse bush, for safety, and left the bikes lying in the dunes, and went down starkers to the shoreline. Neither of us could swim, but we splashed about in the waves.

Then we heard voices shouting, and we could see soldiers with rifles and tin helmets up on the dunes. They had our bikes, and John Coomb, that was my mate, he said, they're shouting at us.

So we waved back, and then they came running down towards

us, leaving the bikes, holding their guns out. You could see their bayonets glinting in the sun, and I thought, they think we're Jerries, because of the bikes being painted black and white.

Then the corporal yelled, Hande Hoch! Fritz. That's how you said hands up, in German, and golly we did, and pretty quick too! So then we tried to explain who we were, and they took us back up into the dunes to find our clothes, but they'd trampled around so much we couldn't find the tracks to where we'd hidden them. Then some more soldiers showed up, and gave us two blankets to wear, and marched us off to the guardhouse.

Anyway, they kept on looking, for uniforms I guess, and found the clothes. We got given tea and crumpets, and put on a lorry, with the bikes on the back and taken home.

The old man gazed around the fields, as if he were watching the German prisoners cutting turnips as they had done all those years ago. He broke into a laugh.

When they finished work for the day, he said, the guards would get them onto the trucks, and then they'd hand up their rifles so they had both hands free to scramble up themselves. They weren't bad men, those Germans.

We're all the same once the uniforms are stripped off, I said thoughtlessly.

Hanley

Hanley shuffled out of the tiny community shop, the carrier-bag bumping his knees as he struggled with the door. He lived in one of the old-folks' cottages.

You'd talk to anybody, Rose said disdainfully. Rose's husband still lectured occasionally, at Cambridge, where they had met. Ellen, whose students had been of all races, creeds and kinds, looked over her glasses.

And why not? Rose stacked shelves and worked the till like a shop-girl.

Well dear, if you don't know by now, it's no use me telling you.

He's retired, Ellen said, like us.

Hardly like us, dear. That was true, Ellen thought; hardly at all.

He had the most wonderful voice. One of the church ladies told Ellen all about him.

Ole Charlie died young, and 'anley's ma got another'un in, and he warn't fer lookin' arter another man's cub, nor 'is own come to that. 'E tole 'anley, sling yer 'uck, an' 'e did. Sleepin' in haybarns, an' sneakin' back 'ome arter the bugger be goin' to work. 'Is ma gev 'im bread an' jam an' sent 'im to school. Never a day did he miss neither, tho' it din't do 'im no good, fer they never taught 'im 'is letters.

She leaned in conspiratorially.

'E 'ad the voice of an angel; still do. They wanted 'im fer Cathedral choir school up city, but who wus gowin' to pay fer the uniform? Besides, he cun't read 'is ABC.

Ellen is on duty. Hanley picks up a ready-meal.

How long would you be a-cookin' summat like this, missus? Ellen takes the packet, hefts it, glancing at the label.

I'd give it twenty minutes, Hanley, in the top of a hot oven. Wait till it's bubbling, and brown on the top.

Ar?

But remember to prick the plastic before you put it in, to let the hot air out.

Oh, ar.

Then be careful opening it. Hanley nods. He's no fool. He thanks her and puts the packet in his carrier. Ellen takes his money and counts out change.

Sing me a song, Hanley.

Hanley glances around. No-one is in the shop. Bob, who was a departmental head at the BBC, is in the stock-room. He falls still, watching through the crack of the half-closed door. Hanley lowers his head, and puts his hands down flat on the counter, the carrier dangling from his wrist. He lifts his head and opens his mouth,

Sweet honey of song flows free and fills the air, resonant, confident.

It is a simple song, in rhyming couplets, telling of starry nights and cold stones, and the warmth of a mother's love. He finishes the song. The sound slips in between the tins and packets squeezed upon the shelves. He smiles, but not at Ellen, and turns away, and nods his head. He carries his groceries out.

Bob breathes again. There are tears in his eyes.

Rose lets everyone believe the misapprehension that arose shortly after she arrived in the village, about her time in Cambridge.

The Loner

There was never anything sexual between them, of that I'm sure. They were close, but they weren't lovers.

I arrived without warning. Work took me past her door. I had no idea he was there. I could she was discomfited, but trying to be polite. She knew me, and spoke my name loud enough for anyone inside to have heard, which in hindsight I realise, was her intent. There was a pause, and I stood there on the doorstep, doubting momentarily that she would invite me in. Then I heard his voice, unmistakable, yet changed, saying, it's alright, let him in.

Then she stepped aside and said, he's through there, pointing to the sitting room.

He was in the armchair, wearing a long dressing gown, which he held tightly around himself with crossed arms. His legs were crossed too, and he wore a pair of battered slippers, and above his bare ankles, and showing quite distinctly below the dressing gown, was the pale blue nylon hem of a women's nightdress. I glanced at her but she simply smiled, and then he said, well, you've finally caught me out after all these years.

She gestured for me to sit down, which I did. I was in a daze. I didn't know how to respond. And it began to dawn on me that what was so surprising was not what he was wearing beneath the dressing gown, but that he looked so relaxed, so completely at ease with himself. He was a changed man.

She said, I'll make us a pot of tea, and bustled out of the room.

He uncrossed his arms and raised his hands in a shrug.

You're a tranny, I said.

No, not technically, he replied with a laugh. I'm a fetishist to be precise, a tactilist some would say.

Isn't that rubber? I asked.

Not for everyone.

We sat staring at each other. He had a curious half smile on his face and the word beatific came into my mind. Then she came back with a tray with mugs of tea and a plate of biscuits on it, chocolate digestives.

I can't remember much about what we said after that. We drank our teas and ate the biscuits, and then I said it was time I went. She got up and saw me to the door. There were no explanations, no excuses or justifications, and I didn't ask for any. I couldn't get over the feeling of calm and peace that flowed out of him. In another situation I might have thought him smug.

We never speak about it. We never have.

On the journey back I realised I envied him. There was nothing I could have done that would have given me such a sense of having become myself. There was nothing I craved for that would have brought me such release. Even if there had been, I knew I had no-one who would have let me share it with such uncritical acceptance.

Small Change

I ran into Billy at a supermarket checkout queue. He was looking older. I said, Billy, remember me? I'd not seen him for years.

He said, Mr D! I've been away for a while. I couldn't see any signs of a tan, but I said, anywhere nice? He said, I've been in Durham, Mr D. And he put a heavy emphasis on Durham. Didn't you see me on the local news? I knew then he didn't mean the Cathedral. Then, while we were waiting for the old lady at the till to sort out her small change and pack her bag, he told me the story.

He'd been on his way back from the supermarket, minding it, weighted down lop-sidedly with a bag of groceries, when he noticed an armoured van parked outside the local branch of a well-known Building Society. Just then a man dressed in uniform with a body-armour vest over, and a visor-ed helmet on his head came out of the Building Society and thumped three times on the side of the van. A metal hatch slid open and a solid looking armoured cash box appeared. The man reached in and took it, and went back inside the branch.

Billy, who'd come to a halt, couldn't help but wonder, what if? And he'd probably never heard of Philip K. Dick. Wouldn't it be amazing, he thought, if he were to bang on the van, and a box were to pop out for him too? In my limited, but hard earned experience of the so-called criminal classes, it's not always the case that crime is genuinely pre-meditated, certainly not planned.

Billy, replicating the rhythm of the security man's knock – Bom, Bom-bom, or Give it *Me*, as it had sounded like to him – banged on the van with his free hand. The hatch, amazingly, shot open and a box just like the previous one appeared. Billy stared at it, and then noticed a man further down the street staring at him. For some reason, that prompted him to act. He grabbed the box, and set off, evenly balanced now, with the groceries in one hand, and the box in the other.

    Billy had never been a particularly athletic youth. He no sooner heard the words, Hey, You! and Stop Thief! than he was floored by several people, including the security guard, and the onlooker. He got four years, it not being a first offence.

By the time he'd told the story, the old lady had gone, and Billy had unloaded, paid for, and was loading his own purchases into two use-again carriers.

    I'm a grandad now, he said, turning to leave. I hadn't known he was even a father. My daughter, he said, tells the boys, your grandda was a bank robber!

    I watched him walk away. At least he was balanced now, I thought, and had no free hands. It's good though, for kids to have someone in the family they can look up to.

Taken

There had been roses in the garden when Granger and his wife moved in. It was their first and only house together. That had been thirty years ago. Granger had loved the roses. Really, they had been what had tipped the balance in favour of the house for him. It had been early spring when they viewed, and late summer when they moved in. The roses had been magnificent that year. Almost every colour of the spectrum was represented, and almost every type of rose. There were climbers and ramblers, and bush roses and double blooms. When the sun blazed and the breeze fell to a whisper, the scent of them sank into the garden like an invisible mist, heavy, heady, pervasive.

Ella had never liked the roses. She could live with them, and as cut flowers, she would agree, they had few competitors. But she did not like the way that they flowered and fell fallow. She did not like the barrenness of their woody stems through the autumn and winter. She did not like the fact that they must be dead-headed, and pruned. Some of them, she complained, flowered only for a week or two, and then only if the weather remained tranquil. Even the rare hot summer would fade them too quickly, and then the pale small petals would fall like, not confetti, but litter. In their decay, she thought, roses were always ugly. In their dormancy, they were like dark, brittle skeletons. And why would anyone need so many?

Their thorns were savage and unforgiving. Their leaves, if they were not nurtured continually, were spotted with black diseases. Insects ate them. They aged badly.

One by one, each with a diversionary excuse, or a promise, was removed from the garden.

Granger had fought the long retreat, bloom by bloom, compromise by compromise, wishing for a longer term gain that never came. There were too many, he conceded. But to one who loved them, that could be no disappointment. He would have wrapped himself in roses. He would have rioted with them like a faun. He would have buried himself in their petals, drowned himself in their perfume, lost himself in their colours. But he had, one translucent petal at a time, relinquished them, like the silky tokens of illicit lovers.

And now the garden was bare but for greenery. Juniperus horizontalis flowed like a cold, grey river along the lawn edges. Columnar evergreens, dark with the shadowing sun, stood like graveyard mutes behind the flower beds. The slight scent of pine, like spilled disinfectant, sometimes wafted to him through the open window.

Sometimes he pondered beginning again, but the sense of loss was greater than the sense of need. He had grown old. Who would share them with him anyway, his revels among the frilled, blousy blooms?

Seemingly By Accident

Fingle was rough with the old man; not actually violent, but he spoke sharply and moved at a speed that was always just a little faster than the old man was comfortable with. Handing him a cup of tea, Fingle would move so fast that however quickly the old man responded he would be conscious of having kept Fingle waiting. Negotiating doors, Fingle would catch his heels or bump his shoulders, always making it appear that the old man's sluggishness, and not his own impatience, had been to blame.

The old man never took his eyes off Fingle, and I was reminded of a farmer who, punching a puppy dog between the eyes without warning, explained that he wanted it always to be paying attention to him.

The old man seemed slower and more stooped each time I saw him, seemed always to be straining to keep up, despite his shuffling, hesitant steps, as if afraid of falling behind; afraid of the consequences he might bring down upon his bowed head. I thought he was getting frailer; that one day Fingle, seemingly by accident, would knock him to the ground; that Fingle's voice, harsh and peremptory, would strike him dumb, and paralysed.

It was when they crossed the road that I feared for him most, for it seemed that Fingle chose to cross when only a precipitous rush would get them safely through the gaps between the speeding cars. I even began to suspect that he was working towards the staging of an incident in which the old man would not make it across.

Perhaps that was why, when I heard about the accident, that I imagined the old man had been knocked down, and it was him I was thinking of when I exclaimed, not killed? It was him I thought of when I was told, no, but he'll be in a wheel-chair for months.

But it was Fingle who had been crippled. Eye-witnesses said that the old man had stepped forward into a gap far too narrow and that Fingle, seeming at first to want to hurry him onwards, had found himself out in front, when the old man, with a nimbleness that had taken the watchers by surprise, had stepped back into safety.

The vehicle that struck Fingle was large, and moving fast. He suffered multiple injuries including several broken bones. It was a miracle, people said, that he had not been killed.

When I saw the pair of them, some weeks after, the old man was walking briskly beside the chair, which was being pushed by a young man I did not recognise. They were negotiating the heavy twin doors into their local pub, trying to manoeuvre Fingle's out-thrust plaster-encased leg and arm through the gap, when the old man, seemingly by accident, let slip his grip on the metal handle. The door swung to against Fingle's foot and he gave a cry of pain. The old man winced, I think.

Innocent Slain!

The pavement ran with blood. That's what the papers said. When I arrived the blood had pooled. As it cooled it dulled, like warm breath condensing on cold metal.

There's a metal smell to blood. I smell it each time I pass the wet brickwork of Cow Tower after rain, following the path he took that night. They intercepted him at Bishop Bridge. I caught up just in time to see him led away. Two policemen held me back. Then I thought of Julie, and ran back along Bishopgate to the centre.

She was dead already. I should have been on time. I shouldn't have given chase. By the time I got back to the scene they'd taken her away. I went to pieces. I've gone over it, and over it.

They took me in an ambulance. Marion came down later for the car, I think. At the hospital they thought I'd been self harming; a man of my age! It was all those little white scars just above the knee. It's a risk of the trade. I've always been a carpet fitter, still am. You spend your life lifting awkward weights, or on your hands and knees, slicing through thick under-felts and rubber-backs with your Stanley knife.

I never saw him again, after that scene on the bridge. He hadn't even glanced at me. I couldn't face the court case. I wasn't needed as a witness. Marion went every day: to see justice done. I didn't care about justice. I just wanted Julie back. That's why she left me, eventually, I think.

I've covered the ground a thousand times since then, ten

thousand. I don't know why. I don't know what I hoped to find, to see. Certainly not him, standing on Bishop Bridge, looking down into the slow, dark water. Surely he couldn't be out? Our lives get longer, but Life gets shorter, shorter even than Julie's.

I knew him right away. He had no idea who I was. I couldn't help myself.

The Wensum, I said, nodding towards the black river.

Yes, he said, and he glanced at me without a flicker of recognition.

You're local? I asked.

Yes, he said, but I've been away for years, working on the rigs. He showed no sign of remorse.

He had a tobacco pouch and started to make a cigarette. The backs of his hands were tattooed. I've been a smoker. I thought, I should offer him a light. In my pocket I felt the slim, ridged hardness of the knife. I don't use Stanleys anymore, but those yellow and black plastic ones with the blades that break off in segments.

He must have thought it was a lighter too, because he turned his throat towards me and leaned in close. Some people ran to help. Others watched. It's all right, I said, he's dead.

As I lifted him, the parapet ran with blood.

Haven

The mist was in when they awoke.

Her back was warm and his half erection nuzzled between her buttocks. She moved gently, like sea wrack against a tide line. He kissed her back. She did not turn but lay facing the viewless window, enjoying the feel of him growing against her.

It's a love story, he said.

What is?

We're writing a love story, being here like this.

Perhaps.

Don't you think so? She slid away from him and rolled onto her back; turned her face towards him.

You can never be sure.

Not of the future, perhaps, but of the now.

You're mixing up love and lust.

Lust is a dirty word, he said.

Lust is an honest word.

I don't feel lustful.

That's because you're sated.

He lifted the duvet and looked down.

You think so?

I think you're being over ambitious, and anyway, it's still lust.

If you say so,

She rolled towards him. They made love again.

The mist filled the sky and clung in tiny silvered drops to the grey, salt sprayed grass. There was no breeze and a slow tide flopped against the foreshore, failing to reach the ragged line of seaweed and debris that marked the previous high water mark.

A cold draught hissed beneath the bathroom door. They had not turned the central heating on. I'm a warm person, she had said.

At lunchtime they walked up through the dunes to eat at the local pub. The mist still hung in the motionless air. It was difficult to judge time without looking at a clock or watch. The tide turned imperceptibly and began to ebb as slowly as it had flowed. There was no breeze. The mist still clung in tiny grey droplets to the silvered grass. The day waxed white and waned grey.

I don't want this to end, he said.

All things end.

Why can't it just go on?

It can begin again, she said. It can repeat itself.

Isn't that the same?

No.

They walked back down through the dunes to the cottage and slipped back into bed. The mist condensed on the viewless window panes. There might be storms far out at sea beyond their seeing.

Two upturned boats lay hauled out upon a mound of grass, their keels like the ridges of windowless, door-less houses, side by side but not toouching.

FINAL MODULE (COLON): *Corporate Training in a Hostile Environment as a Jumping Off Point for Middle Managers Conceptualising Career Re-Alignment & Critical Appraisals* (open bracket) *[SURVIVAL SKILLS]* (closed bracket)

Sam's last job was with a company keen on personal development. They sent everyone on survival courses, with all expenses paid, over weekends in something like a wilderness. These, the personal trainer told them, would be transferable skills.

Where they went, there were no streets full of identical houses. There was no incessant traffic noise or the pollution from a hundred exhaust pipes. There were no concrete underpasses or subways through which icy winds blew, seemingly even on sunny days. There were no dark alleyways filled with discarded cardboard packaging. There were no skips overflowing with out of date supermarket food. There were no inexplicable spaces beneath bridge abutments in city centres where a half a dozen men in sleeping bags could lie side by side with a dog.

There were no strangers with undecipherable eyes looming out of shadows.

Sam learned to make a cosy bed beneath the right sort of

snow, and to scale steep snowfields on mountain sides with the aid of crampons and an ice-axe. He learned to fall from this type of place without killing himself, but instead to tuck his ice-axe into his shoulder and bring his speeding body to a safe resting place.

He learned to track, and to set traps for small game which could be spit roasted or stewed – if you had taken kitchen utensils - over an open fire made from dry wood, taken dead, from the tree and not from the ground. He learned to pee before sleeping to reduce the body's need for energy to keep waste products up to temperature.

He learned to deal with slight hurts that might otherwise get out of hand, such as cuts made with sharp but dirty objects that might fester over weeks if left un-addressed. He heard stories of people who had cut off their own limbs in order to save themselves in desperate situations, people who had cauterised themselves or deadened their wound with fresh ice to numb their pain.

In Sam's last job he learned how to see the way the land lies, and to read clouds foretelling storm, and to negotiate undercurrents or rising tides. He learned to get what he needed from a hostile environment, and to find the right direction when there were none. He learned to have the confidence to rely on himself alone, when it finally came to that, in those sort of situations.

Before Sam's last job came to its end, he had learned to abseil into abysses, although, on that particular day of the course, due to inclement conditions, they trained inside on a wall, using the window ledge high up over a gymnasium to represent a lip of rock.

From that height, onto even a wooden floor with yellow and white lines for games, you would most certainly die. Nobody asked when they were likely to find themselves on a cliff edge, with a handy rope, or, for that matter, at a high window with nobody to talk them down.

3 SITUATIONS
(TEN MORE TALES)

Dawn Chorus

[Jacko said, Let me tell it. I was going to say, but Jacko, it's not your story, but everyone had already turned towards him.]

Billy and Geoff had gone down to London, with a few of the others. They were staying over in somebody's house, so they were on their best behaviour. But the folk they were staying with turned out to be OK. Because no-one had eaten yet they all went down the local pub, which served chicken in a basket which was all the rage in those days.

Now, Billy was having difficulties with his woman at that time, and Geoff was fooling around with anyone, on account of having comprehensively fallen out with his own woman a few weeks before. So, what with the drinks, they were getting on each other's tits. Then Geoff started giving Billy hard beans about the way he was treating Sam – that was Billy's woman – and saying that if he wasn't careful somebody else would do the Doctor John on her, somebody else will, you know? So Billy told him he could effing well have her, and he took himself off into the night.

[It wasn't quite like that, I wanted to say, but it had been a long time ago, and besides, everyone was listening intently. Even one or two of the regulars at the bar, had stopped talking and were looking our way.]

He had no idea where the fuck he was. He didn't know London in those days. So he set off up the street with his bag over his shoulder, and turned left, which he thought must be north, because of the last glimmers of light in the sky. When he got to a big road, he took it. When he got to a little one, he carried on. Eventually he got to a road with road signs, but they were local ones and didn't mean a thing to him, and by that time he had no sense of direction whatsoever, so he flipped a coin. Then he came to a green sign, and he knew where he was heading for.

[I could have corrected him at that point. There was no shoulder bag for a start, and there was no coin. The bag was back at the house. Besides, it's not the events that matter. They aren't the story. It's the significance of the events; that's the story. We were very young at the time, although, of course, at the time, we didn't recognise that. Besides, there's no knowing with father's; when you'll next see them; when you'll see them for the last time. But Jacko was telling the story.]

That was when he started to stick his thumb out, and he got a lift out of the city, that took him to a motorway interchange. Back at the house, they were going nuts. Geoff had sobered up almost immediately, and was feeling bad about what he'd said, and what Billy had done, running out like that. So he got them all to go outside and look for him, even the old couple they were staying with. They were scouring the streets, but it was no good. Billy had got a clear head start, and he wasn't, like they were, going round in circles.

So, Billy was at the motorway, and he had to make his mind up, where, he would tell people who were giving him a lift, he was going. In the end, that was academic, because by the time he did get a lift it was around midnight, and the traffic had slacked off. So, he took the first lift he was offered. The guy had driven up from Dover. He'd driven all the way across Europe, which in those days was an unusual thing. The guy had grabbed a couple of hours sleep and a meal on the ferry, but he was in poor shape for driving. Billy told me, he was driving on the cats eyes between the carriageways, to keep himself awake. Billy was getting tired too by that time, but there was no way he was going to sleep in that vehicle, with the guy touching a hundred on the clock and going thump-thump-thump over the cats eyes with his own eyes still closing and snapping open again every couple of minutes. And the drink was beginning to wear off too, and Billy was beginning to ask himself what he'd got so upset about, and what the hell he was doing in the middle of the night, on the road, with nowhere to go.

The guy who had picked him up was heading for the Midlands, which was where Billy's parents, who were still alive back then, were living, so he decided that was where he'd head for. The guy pulled off the motorway somewhere near Stoke, and then, after a brief period on a dual-carriageway, turned off again onto some minor roads. Then he said, this is where you need to get out.

[We had a similar experience, the two us, a couple of years before it all blew up. We were hitching south then, on a truck with a trailer load of horses, for the Belgian meat trade, the guy said. He smoked like a Victorian factory, and swore like a TV navvy, and you could feel the horses kicking and struggling in the back, and the truck was going from side to side. He said, they keep falling over, but what the fuck. Then he dropped us, in the middle of nowhere, somewhere in Derbyshire, by a concrete bus-shelter. Only there were no buses, and there was no bench in the shelter, so we slept in our sleeping bags on the floor. We would have been better in the open, on the grass, on the verge, that concrete floor was so cold. But we were mates back then, and it was OK. We could laugh about it afterwards. We were going to stay at my folks place, and I remember him walking around the garden with my dad while I watched from the sitting room window, He said, afterwards. Your old man's OK. He never got on with own father.]

By that time Geoff and the others had given up the search, and Geoff had tried to get the old man to ring the police and report him as a missing person, but the old man had said, the Met wouldn't give a tinker's cuss unless you'd been missing for a couple of days, and Geoff had thought about arguing with him, but the guy was like his father, he could see, and once Geoff's father got an idea into his head, however wrong he was, you weren't going to shift it. And Billy had got the wrong idea too, because, Geoff wasn't really interested in his woman, it was just that he didn't like to see his friend losing what he'd got, even if it wasn't such good thing to have right at that moment.

But Billy was in the middle of nowhere, and the guy had driven off into the darkness, chasing his own headlights. There was nothing, except hedges and trees, and a grass verge. There were no houses. There were no street lights. Why the hell the guy had chosen that particular spot to drop him off Billy had no idea. He told me, Jacko, I think the guy had actually gone to sleep and forgotten I was in the car with him, and then when he woke up, he thought, who the fuck is this?

So Billy just stood there, on the roadside. It must have been around two o'clock in the morning by then, and it was pitch black. He could see the stars. Millions of them. And the Milky Way. And he said, there were owls, came out of the trees behind him and flew around his head. He said he stood there for hours, half asleep, not quite awake, with the owls circling his head, like they were trying to work out what he was.

There was no traffic whatsoever in a place like that at that time of the night, at that time of the morning. He stood there until the light started to glimmer again. He stood there while it greyed out the black, until he could see across the fields, and there were the roofs of the houses of a village on another road, and there was the stone tower of a church. And the dawn chorus of the hedgerow birds burst out all around him, and he'd never realised before how noisy it could be. Then he could see sunlight coming up in the east, and the sky was pale and then faint blue and it was going to be a fine day.

And just as he was thinking he might as well stop standing there, because he could see now where he was going, even if he didn't know what it was called, a car drew up alongside him, and stopped, and the driver wound down his window, and leaned over and said, do you need a lift somewhere?

So Billy asked him where he was, and told him where he was trying to get to, and the guy said, he really said this, Billy told me, like in that old music hall joke, if I was going there, I wouldn't start from here.

So the guy gave him a lift down onto the main road where there was a trucker's stop and he walked in there and got a wash in the men's room, and a mug of tea and a bacon banjo, and then one of the truckers gave him a lift onwards to the edge of the town where his parents lived, and he gave them a ring from a phone box, and his old man, whom he hadn't spoken to for about a year, on account of them having had a rough ride over the family business, and him moving away, and then this woman he'd taken up with, and harsh words and all that stuff, his old man came out in the car and took him home.

[It had always been difficult with my dad. We're not always who dads think we are. They haven't always been who we think they were. It's difficult, for some of us, to be sons, and fathers. Jacko knows that. There's a lot I could have asked him, if only I'd known; a lot I could have told him.]

And what with Billy being so tired, and worn down by it perhaps, and hungry too, despite the tea and the bacon butty, he had another breakfast that his mother cooked, and he and his dad had a long talk, and agreed it was all water under the bridge, and that the family business had been a good business to get out of when they had – on account of him not wanting to take it on, and that, until you found the right one, girls weren't worth all that agony, and hassle.

Then, after a big lunch, because it was a Sunday, and because he'd come home unexpectedly, his dad drove him over to the station, and put him on a train back to his own life, and they smiled at each other and shook hands on the platform, like friends. And then, as the train pulled away, Billy watched his dad slip back into the distance.

[Then Jacko turned to look at me, as if to ask, did I do OK? And the others all turned too, but the men at the bar turned away and resumed their conversations. I thought, Jacko you don't know the half of it, but how could he? Neither of us had told him the full story.]

Tears

Will was tearing a small paragraph out of the newspaper, pincering it between the fingers of both hands, tearing neatly, as if down a line of perforations. We have no moral authority to judge the actions of others. We can only guess at their motives. People take us by surprise, and we think that we have misjudged them, unlike characters in stories, whose inconsistencies we put down to bad writing.

He looked up briefly, and then bent back to his task, his tongue pressing against his bottom lip. When the square had come free he folded it in two and slipped it inside his wallet.

I met a woman, I mean, I ran into someone today, Arthur said, who used to be my lover.

Will sat back and waited.

She was older than me, still is, of course. It was thirty years ago. She didn't recognise me at first. We chatted, about this and that. She said, I looked younger. That's why she hadn't recognised me. She looked older, I thought, though I knew her straight away.

You didn't tell her that?

No.

I didn't thank her, Arthur realised as he spoke, for what she had been to me.

Will had been in an institution for a couple of months, but was back living on his own again. Come round for a cuppa, he had said to Arthur. It was his mother, he said, at the root of his problems.

Your mother and I have been friends since she was at school, Arthur said. Acquaintances really. Everyone pussy-footed around Elise's problems.

Will had had to grow up quickly after his dad left. Ringing the ambulance the night Elise had turned left instead of right at the top of the stairs coming out of the bathroom; cleaning the blood off the walls afterwards.

Functioning alcoholics, some people call them. There's nothing to get a handle on with them. They're holding down a job, better than Arthur's in Elise's case. They're contributing to society, paying their way, making themselves useful. It was no use ringing Elise after nine o'clock though, Arthur said. That was when she switched from cider to red wine. Two bottles of the one, one bottle of the other. You need to be successful to afford that sort of drinking every night.

Will had found another snippet and pinched it to a tear, to two tears that spread, neatly, in their appointed lines, right angled, top and side, and then right angled again to the mirror image turn. He slipped it inside his wallet.

You never heard her voice slurred before ten at night, and everything she said, even then, sounded perfectly normal, clever even, perceptive, Elise. She could sort out your problems in a sentence or two, put you on the right lines. Her heart would bleed for you. She would be angry on your behalf. Life is a bitch, she'd say, and she'd kick the bitch for you. The next day though, she'd have no recollection of what you'd said, what she had said, even that you'd spoken together.

Of course I've got a drink problem, she would say, perfectly reasonably, but I've got it under control. She could run rings round you, intellectually, physically. Like bloody Winston Churchill, she could function on four hours sleep a night, and fifteen units of alcohol a day. And if you did cotton on to what was going on, what could you say? What harm could you say it was doing?

She'd been the same since that artist died. Weeping, weeping endlessly for her lost lover, Will said. Will had stuffed his wallet with the tears of newspaper, like small ragged banknotes.

Elise had met that artist only once, Arthur would say, but she'd talk as if they had been best pals. They'd corresponded for years, she said, but Arthur had never seen the letters. He could hardly ask.

It's not normal, Will said, to grieve for someone you hardly knew like that.

Like displaced pain, Arthur thought. He'd heard that she had been raped at university, abused at any rate. It was no more than a rumour someone had queried once.

Wasn't she raped at university, or something like that?

She'd had to take a year off, do it again. That was long before that artist died, though. But it might make you weep, weep endlessly. That might tear something inside so badly that you'd need to drink, or cry. Arthur himself hadn't cried when his father died, until at some other funeral two decades later the tears without warning had flooded out. He remembered the bereaved son, as if offended, saying, what are you crying for, and he, offended too, had replied, don't worry, it's not for your father. Tears were like that. They chose their own time and place.

He should have been at the centre, Arthur thought. Will should have been at the centre of her life. He could not have been expected to stem her weeping, weeping endlessly, though he could not help but try. Arthur, and not only him, might have done more to help, but we are a negative politeness culture, the sociologists say. Who are we to interfere in people's lives if they wish to continue that way?

She'll never be a parent now, sometimes Arthur wanted to say, but who was he to say that? Who were either of them to say? Some people say it is never too late, right up until the moment when it is.

Will's dad was a different man, Arthur said, after he walked out. He still got uptight about Will and his problems though. The boy hadn't turned out the way he'd expected, the way he'd imagined. Other than that, Will's dad was much more relaxed these days. His new woman's daughters treated him like a father.

When Will took out the tears of newspaper to read them the texts were blurred, spotted with his tears.

A Winning

Mervyn was the scruffiest dealer on the circuit, and one of the most hard-working. He wore a pudding-basin hair cut and a brown pullover spotted with moth holes through which showed the pale colours of a vest or T shirt. His shoes were of scuffed suede, and the frayed hems of his non-branded jeans rested exhaustedly upon them. He was a small man, but had none of that aggressive vigour associated with small men. He worked slowly and methodically, and when not working he sat curled up behind his stall listening to rather than joining in with the conversations of the customers who browsed his stock.

I ran into him at fairs from the English Channel to the Scottish Highlands. He used to hire a big white van, one of those with double wheels and a hydraulic lift at the back, and he'd fill it, too. I'd turn up in a small hatchback into which I'd crammed fifteen boxes of second hand books and four folding bookcases. Sometimes I thought the suspension wouldn't stand it. I'd book a six foot stall. He'd have twenty-four feet, thirty if he could get it, and he never had an assistant.

He lived somewhere on the south coast, where I think he had a full-time shop. I'd see him fifty miles north of Edinburgh, already setting up as I arrived. Did you stay over last night? I'd ask. No, he'd reply, I came up this morning. In that van? With all that stock? How? It must have taken hours, all night. He'd drive home too, after the show, breaking his journey at some motorway services or other for a meal.

He was civil rather than friendly and carried his head down, as if he were searching the floor for something he'd dropped. Maybe that's why his face seemed always to be in shadow, though when he looked up to speak, the shadow still seemed to lie within. When there were no customers standing in front of his stall he would busy himself with moving his stock about, shifting it from one place to another without any apparent improvement. He did this slowly and deliberately, as a robot might, without showing any sign of enthusiasm or satisfaction.

I thought he must constantly be tired, wearied by the long slow journeys in the over-stuffed vans and by the repeated setting up and dismantling of his over-large stall. When I imagined him driving through the hours of darkness it was as a creeping sort of beetle, burdened by the oversize carapace of his vehicle.

We were all a little odd, I think, looking back; travelling from one end of the country to another with our cars and vans full of stock, arriving in darkness, leaving in darkness, visiting interesting places, but seeing nothing of them except the interiors of various public halls and sports centres. You could have made a game of it: taking us, blindfolded, to anonymous venues and asking us to guess which part of the country we were in. The accents of the building staffs, and the local people running the refreshments stalls would have given it away, more than those of the punters. The punters were always the same: like minded people, sharing the same interests, dreaming the same dreams.

I liked the punters, mostly. There were some though, who chiselled you down on prices to where you couldn't see the point of doing it anymore. I was trying to make a living, but not everybody was. One of the dealers was a millionaire. It was said that he owned and had restored a chateau in France. He wasn't scruffy, but his stall was. It was full of tat and junk, but in moments of boredom he would break into a market trader's patter, or the caricature of one, and amazingly, people would gather around him.

He owned a factory too, where he manufactured a product which, he told me, he no longer touched or even saw. Once, suddenly fixing me with a penetrating stare he said solemnly and I think without irony: It takes something to make a living out of second hand books. I took it at face value, as a compliment. The last time I saw him he was sporting a huge handlebar moustache which he'd grown for a bit part in a TV period drama.

Mervyn too had another life. In an old coal mining town in the North East, I was given a glimpse into it one slow afternoon when the punters had all vanished but it was too early to think of packing up. At times like that you either sit in gloomy isolation, or, asking a neighbour to keep an eye on your stall, take a walk around the hall to see how the other dealers have done.

I wandered past Mervyn's stall. The shadow was still in his face, but bright eyes glittered from it. He seemed agitated. I gave him the usual rueful smile and made a general enquiry. He was glancing from side to side. I thought of a bird loose in a room.

I've got a horse, he said and his head jerked as if someone had pulled on a rein. In a race, he added, and he lifted his arm and looked at his wristwatch momentarily. The two thirty, he said and he named a racecourse. This was before the days of smart phones and laptops, but he sat with the earplug of a transistor radio pushed in to his ear, and black trailing wires that meandered down into the shadows of empty boxes beneath his tabletop.

You've got a bet on? I said. I've never been into that. I've always been cautious with money.

Four grand, he said.

I couldn't take it in, and repeated the figure back to him. He rattled off some more figures. He might have said, thirty to one. The odds I supposed. It didn't mean much to me, but I knew that was chancey. He fixed me with his eyes as he spoke and held my gaze until I looked away. I looked at my own watch. It was coming to the half hour. They'll be off around now, he said. Four grand was about ten times what I had hoped to take for the day at the fair, at best. I didn't know what to say, and almost staggered rather than walked away from his stall.

Later, as we were packing up, I saw him again. He was looking flushed and excited. It was absurd really, but we always felt under as much pressure to get away quickly at the end of the day as we had to set up in time for the opening. Sometimes it was the caretakers or organisers who put us under actual pressure to clear the building, but there was an underlying, internal compulsion that drove us too. We jostled for the lifts, or impatiently carried down, sometimes several flights of twisting, narrow stairs. We blocked up the loading bays and jammed the car park. It's as if we were somehow afraid of being last out or left behind. It was over, and we wanted it to end. We wanted to be packed back into our cars and vans, and back on the road towards home.

But that wasn't what was driving Mervyn. He was alight. He was more animated than I'd ever seen him. The shadow in his face had entirely burned away. His eyes were like embers. He was switched on, electrified. He'd even lost that scruffy look. He'd come alive.

I raised my eyebrows in question as I passed him. I was carrying two boxes, the upper one pressed against my chin. Over it I saw him. He gave me a beaming smile, and in answer, the merest shake of his head.

The Children's Friend

The last time I saw Harry he was still standing the open market in the square.

Happy Harry's Toy Emporium in rainbow letters dangled from the front of his awning, and Harry's clown face thrust through the narrow gap between two vertical boards to which a hundred different old fashioned tricks and toys were fastened, suspended in little plastic packets from L shaped hooks. There were snakes on sticks, and miniature buckets full of dice, and little bottles reputed to contain 'stink bomb essence – made from drains.' In a corner of the stall a black plastic spider bungeed from a web made of elasticated black string. On the counter below, plastic toy soldiers of different sizes fought a chaotic melee with farm and zoo animals, all mixed up together. There was nothing that cost as much as a pound, and nothing that you could think of that might cost less which wasn't there.

Harry, with a broad red-lipsticked smile and a ping-pong-ball nose on a painted field of white, listed in endless patter all the wonders he had for sale – cheap imports from what was then the reputed source of all badly made tat, Hong Kong. Two stage make-up black crosses were nailed to Harry's eyes, which shone as he pattered. At the ends of baggy green sleeves, his oversized hands in clown's gloves, amazingly, managed to pick up and packet in small brown paper bags the individual items that eager children pointed to, or indulgent parents lifted towards him. The bells on his clown's hat jingled like the small change he shot into his tin. The children's eyes sparkled and their mouths hung open with delight. Harry seemed to like the way they hid nothing of their desires and disappointments; the way their emotions were painted on their faces in all the gaudy colours of his own clown's face. Watching him do the patter I used to think he was getting as excited as they were.

There never seemed to be a moment, on market days, when the stall was not crowded with excited, noisy, jostling children and their slightly agitated, patient parents, and it didn't matter what he was saying or doing, Happy Harry's face always had that wide-eyed big-mouthed smile plastered across it. I never saw him get irritated with the children, even the pushy ones who wouldn't wait their turn and clamoured for his attention. All he'd do, if he wanted to make them wait, was to raise both his big hands and shake them like tambourines, and he'd make an oh-oh-oh noise, as if he was losing control, as if something terrible and shocking was happening to him, as if he was being overwhelmed. That would stop them in their tracks, and then the hands would come down and he'd quietly get on with serving whoever's turn it really was. Even when he looked as if he wasn't, Happy Harry was always in control; he always knew exactly what he was doing. Sometimes, after a little episode like that, he'd hold on to the brown paper bag just a little longer than normal, so that he and the child he was serving would both be holding it, and would be looking into each other's eyes, and then he'd pull a face, or roll his eyes behind the black crosses, and give the tiniest shake of his head, as if he and the child were sharing a secret about the noisy one, who would have fallen silent by then.

His daughter, Scylla stood the market with him in those last months. She had a full time job as a teacher, but he was only doing Saturdays by then, and she came down to help him set up, and hovered in the background while he did his thing. Helped him pack up and put it all back in the van at the end of the day, and wished he'd give it up. But he just loves being with the children, she told me.

And what else would he do? He'd done it for thirty years: the same patter, the same trashy tricks and toys. He'd done it ever since he came out, of the Swiss Navy. They have one, he'd tell you, on Lake Constance. The Bodensee, he'd tell you. That's what they call it. Best posting in Europe, during the war, he'd say, meaning the Second World one. Austria, Germany and Switzerland, he'd say, cut it up between them, used to meet in the middle to swap luxuries, exchange contraband, diplomatic secrets, and he'd he tap the side of his nose with his finger. Nothing you couldn't have read in a book though.

Scylla would take over the stall to give him a break at lunchtime. You need to eat, she'd tell him. To keep you alive, she'd say in answer to his clown's surprised eyes. That's no reason, he'd reply, and she'd say, with two long, sad syllables, da-ad.

The kids around the stall got younger as time went on. Kids

grow up quicker every day. That wasn't all that was changing. Parents started to get fussy, about what things were made of – whether they could be swallowed by mistake – whether the paint was toxic. They started to ask about where things were made, and under what conditions, and some of the toys began to look inappropriate, politically incorrect. Harry answered them all with the same fixed grin. One day a slim man in a suit, poking with his rolled umbrella, took exception to a hangman toy. Harry thought it was a wind-up at first, not the hangman toy. That worked with a little string at the back that you pulled.

The Council took an interest. I've had this pitch for thirty years, Harry said, but that wasn't the point. Besides, as time went on, the number of items you needed to sell at under a pound, well, you couldn't believe it. The nineteen seventies were a nightmare.

You could retire, dad, Scylla told me she had said.

That was around the last time I saw him still doing the open market in the square. I'd been walking past on my way to the bank and cut through, forgetting it was Market Day. I glanced across, and Scylla was standing the narrow opening at the stall.

I asked about her name once. Priscilla, she said. But…It was the spelling that threw me. Dad was always a Homer fan, she said.

Then, as I passed the stall, something made me look, and there was Harry, standing to one side, leaning against the back wall of the Methodist Hall behind the stall. I didn't recognise him at first. He still had on the make-up, but his face, bereft of the animation of his patter, was that of an old, sad clown, and his arms, from which he had drawn those ridiculous clown gloves and the false sleeves to which they were attached, were mottled with blurred tattoos. He had pulled off the jingle-bell hat to expose the stubble of a shaven head. He was smoking a hand-rolled cigarette, holding the thin white stick between two brown-stained fingers; holding it tentatively to his coarsely painted red lips. His nailed-cross eyes had what combat stressed soldiers used to call the two thousand yard stare. He looked like some haggard whore taking a break between fucks.

I had never realised, though perhaps I should have, just how old he was. It seemed absurd that such a tired old man should be out there with the children, selling his trashy tricks and toys behind the mask of his clown's face.

I wrote a story about Harry, not unlike this one, and sent it to an editor. She rejected it, but knowing me well enough to spare the time, told me, it's well enough written, but why would I want to publish a story about an old paedophile? I wondered if she had mixed it up with somebody else's story.

Insubstantiality – an awful tale of the death and afterlife of Samuel Elliston MacGuffin

MacGuffin. Samuel Elliston MacGuffin. That was my name. What more can I say? I was born into a large family in the east end of London during the last quarter of the nineteenth century. We were poor, and unhappy: an unpopular combination with the purveyors of popular fiction.

In my fifteenth year I was lucky enough to find employment in the household of a well to do widow with two young children, for whom I became a sort of unofficial older brother or Dutch uncle. For a decade we lived an idyllic life. I was almost one of the family.

Then the widow remarried. The children were shipped off to a distant boarding school and the house was sold. The entire household was removed to the dour and dismal pile that was Caldthrawn Hall, the ancestral home of Sir Charles Caldthrawn, and the place where my life, as you understand the term, came to its unexpected and untimely conclusion.

Needless, perhaps, to say, for I am sure you are an alert and perceptive reader, but since then I have been the ghost of the man I once was; a state much more common than, I suspect, it is commonly presumed to be, and one into which many have already fallen who have not yet run the final furlong, as I, to all intents and purposes, have done.

This then, though not my entire story, is, as you will eventually realise, an account of what has been, perhaps, its most shocking episode.

The bell hadn't rung for years, though time, I admit, has been somewhat hazy for me of late.

I entered through the bedroom door and appeared before him. I hadn't been back since that night. The room had changed. It was brighter, crisper. They had taken off the old flock wallpaper, or covered it over and the room was now a plain, smooth, creamy white. It had lost that gloomy dampness. They had done something to the windows too. Even the glass seemed somehow different; cleaner, more transparent, and there were two layers of it. Light flooded into the room, even though it was early evening.

They had changed the shape of it too. Some sort of cubicle had been partitioned off at one corner, and the large four poster bed had been replaced with something much plainer. There was a perfunctory table against the wall, with a large but not ornate mirror behind it, and an un-upholstered chair before it. The fire-grate had been taken out and a simple recess put in its place, yet, curiously the room felt warm, as if there were some hidden heat source. Happily, the fire irons were still there, but they were displayed now as if they were an ornament: gleaming and black, with two lamps playing upon them, one to either side at the back of the recess. The bell-pull was the same one that I remembered, the one that he had used to summon me on that evening so long ago.

The man in the room this evening was middle aged, and he had just stepped out of the little cubicle. He was wearing a short robe made of some coarse white material, such as towels are made of. Various items of clothing were strewn about the bed. I could see that they had not been laid out by a proper gentleman's gentleman. He seemed surprised to see me.

You rang, sir? It was good to say the old words again. He seemed confused, and I nodded towards the bell-pull.

That works? He said. I'm sorry, I thought it was just for show. I didn't realise it was connected to anything. Another idiot, I thought. We stood looking at each other. You're in period costume, I see, he said. He meant historical, and I realised that I was. At least, that's the way it must have looked to him.

Is there anything I can get you, sir?

No, look, I'm sorry. I have everything I need. I only pulled it out of curiosity, he said, pointing to the bell-pull.

Curiosity killed the cat, I reminded myself, and would do again. I bowed my head and smiled. It was not my intention to give up my opportunity so easily. Perhaps I might, I said, nodding towards the fireplace, make a little adjustment, while I'm here.

Yes, of course, carry on.

I was glad to see the poker still there. I had often wondered what would become of it. I had not encountered the spirit of Sir Charles since the event. Truth to be told, I had encountered no spirits. That's not the way it works. Had I done so, encountered Sir Charles, I mean, I doubt we would have had much to say to each other. Everything I had wanted to say had been said then, as I stood over him, with the poker in my hand. I have had time to think about it since, and there was nothing that I wanted to add; nothing to un-say either, come to that.

I moved across to the fireplace and leaned in, intending to pick up the poker, when the man spoke again.

That was used in a murder, you know.

I turned around and looked at him.

The poker, he said. Well, I guess you'd already know that, seeing as you work here.

A murder, sir? I feigned ignorance. He brightened up. Perhaps it was the chance to tell the story.

My great, great uncle was murdered, in this very room, by his serving man, with that very poker.

He was, sir?

Oh, yes. It's a piece of family history. Of course, that was in the days when this was a private house. He glanced over to the bell-pull. He'd summoned the serving man using this very rope. Then, and no-one knows why, they must have quarrelled. Anyway, the servant guy, belted him over the head with the poker. Killed him outright.

I allowed my face to express amazement, although I could have carped at that outright, considering.

He swung for it of course, the man said, the servant. By the neck until dead. We still did that in those days.

The memory of the rope, not the bell-rope, flooded into my

mind and for a moment I felt it once more around my throat, and that giddiness after the trapdoor had opened but before I had begun to fall.

I guess the old guy was a bit of a tartar, the man said, to his servants, I mean, but then again, you don't want the servants taking matters into their own hands, do you?

I wished that the man would not use the S word so freely. It irritated me. And now that he had spoken of the incident, revealed his identity, I could see the similarity, of features and demeanour between him and old Sir Charles, who, it must be said, in all fairness, was not so much a tartar as an entire and unmitigated tyrant, who deserved everything that he got, and was lucky that he had not got it sooner.

Of course, the man went on, that doesn't justify the assault. I've no doubt he was just trying to keep his man in his proper place.

His proper place, sir?

Well, he said, servants presume. They become over familiar. They start giving you advice, well meant, no doubt, and sometimes, perhaps, very good advice, which you appear to accept, having come to similar conclusions yourself. But the next thing you know is, they're telling you how to run your own business. They're telling you how to live your life. It's not all Jeeves and Wooster out there in the real world.

Indeed no, sir. The amazed expression on my face must have changed itself, for he suddenly looked concerned.

No offence.

None taken, sir, I dissimulated.

That's the reason I asked specifically to stay in this room, he said. I pulled an enquiring expression. Because of the murder, he explained. Today is the anniversary, he said.

It's the 23rd of April? I said, without thinking.

That's right, he replied, without realising. It happened one hundred years ago to the day.

As I told you, I have a very hazy notion of time these days. Even the word 'days' means less and less to me as time, presumably, rolls on. The years flow one into the other. The minutes stretch out into eternity. Another year gone by! A hundred years gone by? I was amazed. Then again, he might have said five hundred and I wouldn't have been any more surprised. Then a penny, or whatever they use these days, dropped.

Say, how did you know the date?

I couldn't keep the smile off my face at that, but stood there grinning at him, and that, I think, must have been when he noticed that slight transparency about me. It's nothing to do with practice or competence, or trying hard. It's simply the way I materialise. Don't ask me if it's the same for the others. I presume there are others, though, as I said before, I have never met any. For me though, there is always that slight insubstantiality. I can detect it myself. If I hold my hand out in front of me I can see a vague wateriness around the edges. If I look down at my waistcoat I get a sense of something empty beneath it. In bright lights the effect is even more noticeable, and the room, that evening, was very bright. My grin broadened as I saw his expression change.

My God! He said, and there was something in the intonation of his voice that brought his great, great uncle back to life, and I felt that same old anger that I'd felt back then. He raised a hand, the finger outstretched, pointing towards me.

You're....he said.

And so I was! I spun around, back towards the fireplace, and snatched for the fire-irons. I'd beaten the brains out of one of his wretched brood before, and I could beat them out of another now. I hadn't felt so fired up for years. I hadn't felt so fired up for a hundred years.

I could feel the taut skin of my face I was grinning so hard, and my open hand slashed down towards the poker handle. I'd smash this one's head in too before he could utter another word.

But there was nothing there! My hand whizzed through the iron poker handle and came out on the other side. It smashed into the wall of the fireplace, but I felt no pain. It passed through that too, and I spun around, losing my balance as it came out through the wall, still open, still moving. I felt myself tumbling forward and put out my other hand to save myself, fell into the recess, through the fire irons and into the floor beneath. I thought I might carry on falling forever, tumbling and turning, to God knew where, but then, behind me, I heard something that brought me to a stop with all the force of a real body landing upon a real stone floor.

He was laughing! Behind my back. He was hooting and

howling and dancing with glee.

I gathered myself up, and pulled myself free of the floor and of the fire-irons, and of the fireplace. I struggled to my feet. Then I dusted off my trousers and pulled down the tails of my waistcoat, and smoothed my hair into place. I stepped back into the room with as much dignity as I could muster, raised an eyebrow and put on my most severe face.

I'll be leaving you now, sir, I said.

Here, he said, and I could see the tears at the corners of his eyes as he struggled to keep control of his voice. Take this, and he tried to push a folded banknote into my hand, but it passed straight through and fluttered gently to the carpet, AS HE KNEW IT WOULD!

Henry and Mr Oufle

Mr Oufle was a cheerful fellow, a rare bird in the dour redbrick town. He liked to have fun with his friends and neighbours, and when he parked his car nose first to the window of the fancy dress shop, he could not help but notice the costumes on display, nor to speculate about how they might be put to use.

In particular he noticed, in the week that the circus was in town, that they had put a man sized grizzly bear suit in the window, and it was this that persuaded him to do more than look. He went into the shop, empty handed, and came out with a bulky package wrapped in a black plastic bin liner.

Mr Oufle and his wife, that night, were joining friends for dinner at a local pizza place. It was a friendly restaurant, noisy and boisterous, just the place, Mr Oufle thought, to spring a grizzly bear on the crowd; especially with the circus being in town.

The Oufles were regular diners at the restaurant, so Mr Oufle had no problem in coming to an arrangement with Charles, one of the waiters, Half way through the evening, when already, perhaps, he had taken more to drink than was wise for a man of his age, Mr Oufle was allowed to slip out through the fire exit, under cover of a trip to the loo. A few minutes later, for the car park was only around the corner, Charles allowed him back in, this time carrying a bulky package wrapped in a black plastic bin liner.

The package was hastily stored in one of the cubicles in the gents, and Mr Oufle rejoined his friends. There was a little preparatory work to do before he reappeared in ursine guise.

You were a long time, his wife observed. Are you alright?

Perfectly well, he said, his face beaming. He poured himself another red wine. They ate nosily and with their fingers. They spoke with their mouths full. They talked across each other. They were the noisiest table in the room, which, as a matter of pride, they always were. Mr Oufle became involved in a heated discussion over the merits, and demerits of the circus, which was in town. Animals in cages, his friends were asserting, was cruel, let alone forcing them to do tricks. He had initiated the discussion to arrive at precisely this point. What, he had planned to say, if one of them were to escape! But when the moment came, having lubricated his arguments with several more glasses of the rather nice merlot, which had slipped down, as they say, like a pair of silk knickers, he forgot entirely why he had engineered the conversation in the first place. The grizzly bear suit had slipped his mind as completely as a real bear might have wanted to slip its cage.

Then it was time to leave. The waiters were helping them on with their coats, and ushering them, grateful for the shift to be drawing to its close at last, out of the door, which snicked to, definitively behind them. Which was when Mr Oufle realised that he needed the loo once more, and remembered the black plastic bin liner.

I need to go back, he told his wife.

Don't be silly, she said.

But I need a pee.

You can pee in the car park, she said. No-one will see in the darkness. Pee between the cars.

The car park was only around the corner. The restaurant door was clearly locked and bolted behind them. The lights were already off. Mr Oufle's shoulders sagged. He sobered a little. What could he do?

The car park was at the edge of the playing fields upon which the circus sat, and as Mr Oufle relieved himself in the dark shadows between the cars, open doors to either side shielding him from view, he stared down towards the big top. There were few lights left on at this time of night, but small red dots buzzed like fireflies around the periphery of the big tent. It was smokers, he realised. He emerged from the canyon and stood with his friends.

Something's going on down there, they said. There were torch lights too, he realised, little daggers of pale yellow that stabbed here and there around the circled trucks and trailers of the circus convoy, behind the wire mesh of its temporary stockade.

They are searching for something, someone said.

Perhaps it is a bear, Mr Oufle said, sadly, thinking of his missed opportunity.

Now Charles, back at the pizza place had been trying to recall precisely what it was he had forgotten in the hectic rush to get Mr Oufle's party out of the door. He knew there was something. Of course. The black plastic bag. A present, perhaps, for someone. It had been left in the gents. He went down to retrieve it, and could not resist looking inside the bag. A pair of black eyes looked up at him from behind a hard black protruding snout.

When the bear came shambling around the corner, on all fours, onto the car park Mrs Oufle saw it first and screamed. Mr Oufle turned, momentarily astounded. The bear came to a halt and rose up on its hind legs. It was a man sized bear. It clawed the air, opened its mouth, revealing shiny white teeth, and gave a roar.

Marvellous, Mr Oufle thought. Exactly as I would have done. Charles, he told himself, had saved the day.

Have no fear, Mr Oufle cried, I shall save you, and he stepped forward to meet the animal. Down at the big top, the red dots and stabbing yellow beams had frozen, momentarily at the sound. As Mr Oufle closed with the bear and attempted to grasp its clawed arms in his own, they began to flow up across the night dark grass towards him. The friends of Mr Oufle, clustering behind their cars had begun to scream. The bear, breaking free with one hairy foreleg fetched Mr Oufle a tremendous biff across the shoulder, which, perhaps because of the alcohol, he withstood.

Steady on old chap, Mr Oufle cried, struggling to keep his feet. The red dots and the torch beams, accompanied now by dark, simian shapes, swarmed over the playing field fence. They too were yelling. The bear and Mr Oufle struggled valiantly before them, neither giving ground.

Stand aside there, a voice said, and Mr Oufle heard the phut of a properly opened champagne bottle, and felt the whizz of something pass his ear, and then the bear went unaccountably feeble, and wobbly, and floppy, and became disinterested in their game, and fell to the ground.

It'll sleep for hours now, the voice said, and a man with a short rifle stepped forward into Mr Oufle's line of sight. But Mr Oufle paid him no heed. He sank down next to the bear and began pulling at its ears as if he were trying to pull off its head entirely.

Charles, Charles, he was calling in desperation. Which was when Charles appeared, from the pizza place, with, in his hand, the black plastic bin liner.

It's perfectly alright, the man with the rifle said, and its name is Henry.

[Inspired by Abbe Boudelot's story, Monsieur Oufle]

The Hotel Ent*rance*

I don't believe in ghosts, I said.

So how do you explain it? He raised a quizzical eyebrow.

The fact is, whatever you don't understand, because you aren't in possession of all the facts, seems like magic, or the supernatural, I told him. Then I went on to recount some examples I'd read of in books, about people with extraordinary abilities, like that kid who could see the reflection of shapes drawn on cards in the eyes of the person who was asking him the questions. He didn't even know he was doing it, I said, but he only got the answers right when the light was in the right position, and the researcher was looking at the pictures.

The guy in the ghost suit rolled his head from side to side, and I could see from the expression on his face he wasn't convinced. I have to say, I didn't like that head rolling, especially when he rolled it from one hand to the other. He tucked it back snugly under his arm.

So how do you think I'm doing this?

I don't know, I said, but it's got to be one of those Darren Brown type tricks.

You think so?

Look, I said, if you'd really pulled your head off, there'd be blood all over the carpet. I splayed an open hand down towards our feet. The carpet was worn. It was a little grubby too, to be honest, but there was no blood. He pulled a lop sided grin, took his head in both hands, and lifted it back onto his shoulders.

I can see I'm wasting my time, he said.

Look, I said. I give you full marks for trying. It can't be easy these days, what with all the CGI and special effects. The problem is we've seen it all before. There's nothing new under the sun. He shook his head, in sorrow and disbelief I guess, and it wobbled precariously, which I thought was a rather a nice touch. Then he started to fade away. I could see he was disappointed. I'll still pay the bill, I said. You guys have earned your money. I don't feel cheated at all. I tried to reassure him, but as he vanished into thin air and I found myself staring at the bare wall once more, I could see there was a look of unhappiness upon his ghostly white face.

It's OK! I said tilting my head up to the ceiling, which is where I guessed the sound system must be located. I've had a great evening. It's been fun.

Of course, there was no response. They could hardly let on. It would have spoiled the illusion, even though they must have realised by then, that as far as I was concerned, that's all it was, just an illusion.

After that it was just an ordinary night, in an ordinary, if somewhat run down, hotel. I confess, I was a little worried about the possibilities of hidden cameras. I mean, I sleep raw, you know, but I kept my boxers on that night, just in case. The fact is, what they really needed, rather than trying to sell themselves as some spooky niche-market venue, was to spend some money on general refurbishment. It wasn't as if they were even marketing themselves effectively. I hadn't stayed over on account of knowing it was a haunted hotel. As far as I could tell they weren't making anything of it. They weren't promoting it. They hadn't even added a premium to the price, although you could argue that the place would have been overpriced at any price, considering the state of the décor.

I'd only stayed over because I'd been on the road all day, and had obviously missed my turn somewhere around Brig O' Whatsitsname, because the road had been getting narrower and narrower for the last few miles and was obviously going nowhere. And then, with the weather closing in like that, well, I just needed a place to stay. It wasn't the fact that the sign board, which, let me tell you, could also have done with a lick of paint, proclaimed it to be *The Haunted House Hotel*, that drew me in. It was the fact that it was any damned Hotel by the time I'd got that far.

And when the bell-pull came off in my hand and I was standing there on the doorstep, in the mist, listening to that foghorn chime that seemed to be coming from the bowels of the earth, and I've got a yard and half of rusty wire in my hand and a hole in the wall that looks like you can see to eternity through it, that's when it hits me: what the name of the game is.

You have to give it to them, the phoney bell-pull was a masterstroke, and the creak on those door hinges when the old guy answered was just pure Hammer! But, and I was thinking this at the time, it's all been done before. I mean, there's nothing new about it. OK, it was fun. The old guy was fun, but they could have gone a bit lighter on the musty smell, particularly when he was serving dinner; which, I must admit, did look like fricassee of corpse, and the pink sauce with it, well. It was salty.

But there's a point when playing the game becomes a little tedious. I'm all in favour of thoroughness. I work in the movies, well, we finance a couple of studios, so I know about back projection and green screens and stuff, and I'm as much a fan of good prosthetics as the next man, but to be honest, all I really wanted was a bed for the night, and a good night's sleep. You can overdo the cobwebs and the dead spiders, you know.

And what's it all for, if you haven't got your advertising right? Have you ever heard of this place? What they should have had, at the very least, was a big new sign on the turn off from the main road; and some leaflets or cards on the reception desk that you could take. And what about wi-fi? If they had it, they weren't letting on. And of course they had it. If you have the technology to project the "ghost", and here I'm holding up the fingers of my two hands and waggling them to represent inverted commas, if you have that sort of technology, you certainly are not going to be without the wi-fi. I mean, they did it very well, but if you haven't got any customers, what's it all for?

I mean, I was the only paying guest in the place that night, and I'm not surprised. Nice try guys, but that ain't the way to run a business.

So when I drove past a couple of days later on my way back, I wasn't surprised to find the place had closed down. What did surprise me, was how quickly they'd cleared the site. I mean, it wasn't just the old sign had gone. The whole building was missing. You couldn't even see where it had stood.....

First Foot

    I had a Scottish friend, in Carlisle once. She was a Socialist, an intellectual. Yet at New Year, which she called Hogmanay, she was very superstitious about who she would let over her threshold for the first time after the hour had struck. I remember her turning away a dog-faced, pale-skinned orphan once. Don't you bring your muddy paws across this threshold, she said, trying to make it sound like a joke, but meaning it. When I think of Henry, I always remember her too.

I'd called Henry on his mobile just before midnight, so it was still New Year's Eve. I suppose I felt responsible, for having encouraged him.

    He-lo-immy.

    I said, you're breaking up, Henry.

    Ho-don-imm. Then he came through clear and strong, and we wished each other a premature happy New Year. He said, I've come upstairs to the bedroom. It's the only place I can get a decent signal up here. He told me the weather was good: a starry sky and snow on the ground, but he sounded tense, and there was a howling in the background that worried me.

    Is everything OK? I asked him. You sound a little strained.

    I'm great, he said. Then he said, I had a run in with the neighbour. I told him, keep your dogs under control, and he said he hasn't got any dogs.

I wondered if this was the time to tell Henry what I'd found out, about the house, but he hadn't finished telling me yet. He said, I know damned well he's got dogs. I've been finding their tracks in the snow around the house for the last couple of mornings, and you can hear them howling all night long.

I'd talked to the locals, in the pub. They told me the story. Some black-shirted fascist had lived in there during the nineteen thirties. The fascist had a German Shepherd dog, named Adolf. That was all the rage those days, among fascists.

Henry had bought the house back in the nineties. Property prices had taken a nose-dive. It'll only be temporary, Henry said. That wasn't the point though. He loved the place. He and Miriam went up every year and stayed the summer. Easter till All Souls. I don't think Miriam was all that fond of it, but Henry would have stayed the year round if he could. He said, maybe, if Miriam isn't too upset about it, I'll stay over one winter on my own.

I said, just do it, while you've got the chance. I mean, what else was I going to say to him? I hadn't heard the story by then.

He said, why don't you come up with me and stay for Hogmanay?

What do I want with porridge and bagpipes?

You might like a wee dram, he said.

And there was a gardener in the story. Perhaps he was some kind of leftie-intellectual, or gay, or Jewish. Well, this gardener, he subverted the dog. He taught it to respond to the name Schicklegruber. That's what Adolf Hitler's proper name was. So when the gardener called out, hey, Schicklegruber, here, boy! the dog would come running. When he said, Schicklegruber, die for your country! the dog wouldn't roll over. This gardener had a sense a humour; and people say the Scots are dour. He says, Schicklegruber, Die for your country, and the dog covers its nose with its paws and whines. Isn't that some trick?

It was what they call a bothy up there, with small square windows deep-set in thick walls and the bedrooms pushed up into the roof space with crooked little garret windows, and the chimneys capped with slates. Henry told me it hadn't been lived in since before the second world war, because it had no running water, or sanitation, or electricity. That didn't put him off though. He said, we can do the place up like new, and that's what he did, though it took him a while, and they wouldn't let him mess with the outside because of their Scottish heritage.

They're so laid back up here, he told me, except when you want to make something better. I went up early in the new millennium. He'd been nagging me for years, and I could see he was hurt that I wasn't up for it. So I went up with Bob and Doreen.

We flew to Glasgow in midsummer. You'd never have guessed. It was fifteen degrees and cloudy, and the tarmac was wet from recent rain. I said, is this the best they can do for a summer?

and Bob told me I should think myself lucky.

We had a great time though, despite the weather. We stayed a week or two. I slept downstairs on a folding bed in front of the open fire. That was cool. There was only one extra bedroom upstairs and it would have been churlish not to let Bob and Dee have it. I rather liked the place. Sure, it was cold and dark, but it was a proper old-fashioned Scottish house.

Jody has stayed there. She just loved the place, Henry said.

I never thought any more about it, till I was talking to Jody, about the time she stayed. I asked her, what did you think of the place? She said well, don't get me wrong, I had a great time up there, but the house itself, it was kind of creepy.

Creepy?

She said, you know. It had that atmosphere you get sometimes. I said, did it? She said, it certainly did? Didn't you feel it, when you stayed? Well, I couldn't say that I had, except for getting a cold shiver every time I went along the corridor to the bathroom upstairs, but they've got rudimentary heating up there, and no insulation and you know what Jody's like. I would have left it at that, except that I ran into Bob and Dee a couple of months later. They told me that Henry had finally decided to take himself off and stay the year round in his Scottish house. He would be spending his first New Year there in a few weeks.

I asked them, did you like the place? They said, we liked the countryside, but the house itself... Then they made sheep's eyes at each other.

What? I asked.

Didn't you feel it? Bob asked

. Feel what? I said. I don't get this atmosphere stuff.

In that little room we stayed in, Dee said. Well, it was, you know, creepy.

Creepy? I said. What does that mean?

Like someone had been ripped to death in there, Bob said.

Then, a couple of days before New Year, the fascist finds out, about the Schicklegruber trick. He goes ape-shit, but he doesn't take it out on the gardener. He takes it out on the dog and beats it to death with a spade. Then he gets the gardener, who must have been feeling pretty guilty by that time, and tells him to bury it in the cellar. The ground outside must have been too hard to dig.

But there isn't a cellar at the house, I said. That's because they've bricked it up. After they told me that, I wasn't so keen on sleeping down there, by the open fireplace, for a couple nights, but, hey, there was no growling and scratching at the floorboards that I could hear, so after a while I gave up worrying. Besides, it was nowhere near Hogmanay. I said to Henry, have you heard what the locals are saying about this place? But Henry doesn't go down his local, because he brought in the builders from outside.

I should have told him then.

The internet is wonderful thing. You can find out almost anything you want. I did a little surfing. The story of the dog was there okay, every grisly detail, but the locals hadn't told me everything. Not only had the fascist guy beat the dog to death, but in the early hours of New Year's Day, something had crept into his bedroom and attacked him in his bed and torn his throat out. That was why the place had stood empty for so long. No one in his right mind, it said, would stay there nights over Hogmanay.

Then I could hear the clock chiming, down his mobile, and Henry said, it's striking twelve. It's New Year's Day! I said, Henry, there's something I've got to tell you, but he said, it'll have to wait Jimmy, I've got to go, they're rattling the door down there, but Happy New Year, and he cut off.

The Silence

A long time ago, when Ray started at the quarry, he couldn't even budge the sacks of sand and gravel let alone lift them. He couldn't even get the crowbar underneath the boulders let alone budge them. He tangled the chains and couldn't grip the links that slid through his fingers, stripping skin. The other men in the crew would stand and watch him, laughing; but they said nothing and never offered to help. It was fifty percent technique, but he had to find that out for himself. Ray grappled and pulled and heaved and shoved and wept while they looked on, and after they'd moved away to get on with their own work.

It wasn't that though. He learned to curse the sacks and to throw them like corpses onto the flatbeds of the trucks alongside those of the other men. He learned to tell by their shapes which way the boulders would roll or tumble, the angles of their centres of gravity. All of them were predisposed to topple in some particular direction. He learned to lever them just so, but still it would take only just a little less than everything he had to give to shift them onto the waiting scoop of the front loader. He learned to swing the chains and loop them like a coil of rope.

It was the silence of the other men that he had no techniques for dealing with, neither to break nor to endure. For they did not speak, neither to him nor to each other, but worked in silence, sat in silence, even during the long drawn out hour of the lunch break.

Each one in his separate place with his flask and sandwiches. None of them took a magazine or a newspaper. None of them brought in a radio. They spoke of nothing they had seen or heard or done: no sport, no hobby, no antics of children, no politics, no domestic quarrels, no pleasures or pains, no fears or hopes, no sexual exploits. They had nothing to report, and greeted his attempts at conversation, his good mornings and good nights, with baffled, silent incomprehension, with hostility. It was as if they spoke a foreign language, except for that they did not speak at all, as if words might dislodge an avalanche of angers, recriminations, frustrations, resentments, which once started no-one might stop.

Above the fresh peeled skin of the quarry face curlew called as they climbed the sky to glide down again, and lapwing swung like kites on tugged strings, and the wind sung a low harmonic through the bristle grasses.

The men sat in the slate-walled, slate-flagged, slate- roofed crew room and drank their drinks and ate their food like shedded cattle chewing cud, not even responding when one spilled a drink or dropped a sandwich, though they would watch with slow unblinking eyes. The second week he took in a book; read it at the morning break and at mid-day. They watched with disbelief, trepidation even, as if he had carried in among them an unexploded bomb. They watched as if watching enough might make it disappear, and he began to think that they watched everything that way: him, themselves, the sacks, the boulders, the trucks. But he could never tell whether they watched in hope or in fear of such disappearing. And the last man out swept clear the room of the dust and debris that was left behind them, which the wind lifted at the door step and carried away.

The work was hard and unremitting and each man found his own pace that he could sustain until the job was done. Their hands were rough and hard, never mind the thick gloves they wore, which in any case were threadbare and holed at the finger ends. They wore thick trousers and corduroy jackets. It was before the days of fluorescent tabards and company issue safety boots, and orange plastic helmets, so they wore on their feet what they had and went bareheaded. Pale dust of the pounded stone settled on them, making their dark clothes dirty white and circling their eyes and coating their tongues, and sometimes they coughed and spat into scraps of cloth that once had been handkerchiefs, which may have been why they did not speak.

They take some getting used to, the foreman had said, and he didn't speak much either, save to order them to move this or shift that while the day lasted, before vanishing among the pyramids of sacks, the hills of chippings and slag, the jumbles of boulders, on errands of his own. And, watch out for Gorach, he said, he can be awkward since his girl left him.

Gorach came over after the lunch break when only he and Ray were left in the crew room, and stood with his legs apart over Ray where he sat reading his book.

What d'you bring that fucking thing in for? Ray looked up and closed his book.

I'm reading it, he said.

I can see that, Gorach said.

It's a book of short stories, Ray said.

Stories are for kids.

I like them too.

You're fucking weird, Gorach said. Ray opened the book again and continued to read. I said, you're fucking weird, Gorach repeated. Then Ray closed the book and slipped it into his jacket pocket and stood up. His face was only inches from the other man's.

You have no idea how fucking weird I am, he said.

And that was true.

Then Ray seemed to be about to step forward and Gorach moved aside and as Ray passed him Gorach said, I could fucking break you with one hand behind my back, and Ray, stopping and turning at the door, said, and what difference would that make?

After that nothing was said for several days, but the silence had been changed. Nobody looked at anybody else anymore, except at Ray, who still said good morning, and good night, and, if he had to infringe or intrude upon somebody's personal space, which was always bigger than you might expect it to be, he would say, excuse me.

Then Gorach told everyone to fuck off, half half-way through the lunch break one day and said, not you, to Ray who had begun to stand up. Ray had been reading his book, which he slipped into his pocket and stood with his hand on waiting for Gorach to say more. Then Gorach handed over a small blue envelope which had been opened but which still had the folded letter inside, and said, read this for me, and, if you fucking laugh, I'll kill you.

A sack wouldn't do you much harm unless somebody swung it at you and knocked you off your feet into the path of something, or over an unprotected edge, but if one of the boulders, which were used for ornamental rockeries, or to fill steel cages as rock armour, or to close off lay-byes and entrances to tracts of land upon which motor vehicles were no longer permitted, if one of them fell upon you, it could crush a hand or foot or even a leg, and you might find yourself unable to work for months, or even years and, back then, with no hope of compensation unless you could prove it had been somebody else's fault. And when Ray saw such things happen, he turned away and nodded his head, but said nothing.

So Ray took the envelope and removed the letter and unfolded it and read it silently, before refolding it and slipping it back inside the envelope, which he handed back to Gorach.

And he didn't laugh at all, but turned away and left the crew room, and Gorach, holding the envelope in his hand, watched him go.

Clicks

Everywhere's three clicks away these days, Jack Fallows had said, leaving. He meant online.

Guy watched the taxi recede into the distance of the long straight road to the airfield. Gretchen turned away murmuring something in Dutch. Guy had never bothered to learn Dutch. He hadn't needed to; but over the last couple of years Gretch had fitfully reverted to her first language.

Jack had been one of the first to visit them. That was nearly a decade ago. Jack's wife had still been alive back then and they had driven up together all the way from London. He had pointed to the tangle of overgrown shrubs that masked the front of The Bothy.

Windbreak, he had said. Guy still had no idea what they were called, but he had grubbed them all out to reveal the view. He had planted box instead, which he had expected to grow to four feet within ten years. That would have provided a measure of protection, and allowed you to stand in the new conservatory and look out over the gently sloping hillside down to the coast and the burnished steel bay beyond. Eight years on and the box was barely two foot high, and individual plants had succumbed. At this rate, Guy told himself, I'll be in my eighties.

Jack's garden at Winterbourne Cottage nestled in to a narrow groove that was padded with Azaleas and Rhododendrons; not common ponticums, but species plants that flowered in subtle colours and had spectacular foliage all year round. They had leaves the size of dinner plates or like oversized spear heads of beaten copper. He was three hops away from the city: a short car ride, a local train, the tube; tried to get to a show once a month, to galleries, museums. He even went in to some poetry event, or was it fiction, at some pub in Soho. There was music here too, and poetry, but Guy always felt uncomfortable, elbow to elbow in the tiny room while the band played – none of them looking younger than seventy – a table top their stage, amplifiers tucked underneath, and them sitting in a square with the crowd at their backs. Gretchen had discovered that her ancestors, from Rotterdam, had traded in the islands for fish, centuries back.

Guy looked at his watch. Duncan would be arriving soon for a coffee. Duncan was not a local, though he lived only a mile or two away.

He's like yourself, mm, yes, the postie had said. He blew in a few years before you. He's a Scot, a Lewis man, from Stornoway, yes.

Everybody had come to visit that first summer, before even the building work was finished, but Guy and Gretchen had managed. It had been one long party. Over the years though, it had tailed off. It was difficult to get to from London. Even the kids came barely once a year and they jetted off all over the world. They could skype from anywhere. By car it took the best part of two days, if you made an early start, and by train you could get only as far as Glasgow. After that it had to be a hire car or fly in. Even if you flew to Glasgow you'd need an overnight. None of them were getting any younger, their city friends.

They'd put in a wood-burner. Absurd. There were almost no trees on the islands: a few in walled gardens or in deep, sheltered valleys. . There were those scrubby shrubs, like the ones he'd dug out. The long low houses hid behind them. They seemed dark and dusty, as if they caught the fine sand blown up from the beaches. He'd had to have it brought in, firewood; dumpy bags full of chopped logs, neat as building bricks. They'd emptied them out and re-stacked them along the side of the house that first year, but after that they had left them in the bags. Old plastic fertilizer sacks cut open and spread on top to keep off the rain.

Eventually they'd given up altogether, relied on the oil-fired central heating, put dried flowers in front of the stove

They'd made a killing on the house, compared to the cost of The Bothy, but whereas that had stayed at around the same value, even with all the work, to buy back near to London, they'd have to pay ten times as much.

Everything was barren in the winter. Guy looked out over the bare hillside towards the tarmac ocean. There had been forests of people in the city. Rivers of pedestrians had cascaded down The Strand and into the whirlpool of Trafalgar Square. He remembered the streams of people flowing across Blackfriars Bridge in the mornings and in the evenings: suits and black bowlers, umbrellas and briefcases, and the black cabs buzzing like bees; tourists making jazz-hands for photographs in front of the posters outside The Aldwych.

You'll never guess who I ran into on the terrace at Somerset House, Jack had said. That fellow off Gardener's World. Charming man. I asked him about the Rhododendrons at the cottage. Very helpful.

Guy remembered the last time he and Gretch had revisited. What a palaver! But worth it. They'd stayed on The Strand. They'd seen that actress, what's her name, who'd been in the sit-com. She'd been walking past Horse Guards parade, as cool as you like and looking half her age. And the restaurants: so many to choose from; the street entertainers at Covent Garden.

The buzz. The buzz of the hive. It was the people he missed; not the people he knew, but the strangers, talking in their hundred different languages, with their thousand different accents, wearing their different clothes: keeping themselves to themselves, passing you by. Yet, every now and then, in among the crowds, you'd catch an eye, a face that seemed to say, I know you! You know me! We're alike, we two, among these strangers here. We know. The knowing look of a man or woman – didn't matter which – that said, we belong here; doesn't matter when we came, or where from, or how long ago. We're the same, you and I. And then you'd pass on into the crowd.

4 MILDRED'S RECOLLECTIONS (OF *THAT* KOWALSKI)

Kowalski Italian

That Kowalski. I sends him ta do tha shoppin'. We's havin' Sharon an' Joe round fer an Italian evenin' on account a her ethnicity. I gives him the list, but as he's gowin' out the door I remembers the breadsticks.

I says, an' get us some Grissini, Kowalski. He says, sure thing Mildred.

So, he's comin' 'ome two hours later wid the carrier bags. He puts 'em down onya table an' pulls a cd out uv his coat pocket.

He says, I cu'nt get no Grissini, Mildred, so I brung Pavarotti instead.

Whaddya gonna do with 'em?

Kowalski Poppin'

That Kowalski. Ain't he the living proof a man needs a hobby? Cause if'n he ain't got a hobby, sooner or later he's gonna come around lookin' fer ta help ya in the house. You ain't got no idea how many ways he's gonna come up with ta mess up what ya doin'.

So, I'se strippin' the bed in tha guest bedroom on account we just got shut ov a guest, and that Kowalski, he comes wanderin' in lookin' forlorn. He says, Mildred, ya wan I should help ya? I says, Kowalski, ain't ya got some pressin' woyk a ya own, like watchin' sumpin' important on ya TV? He says, Mildred, they ain't nuthin' on woyth watchin'. He's a discernin' viewer, is ya Kowalski. He says, Mildred, they mus' be sumpin' I can do gonna make ya life a little easier. So, when I'se finished runnin' through tha list in my head, I says, Kowalski, why doancha take the cover of'n that duvet?

Whaddeye should a said was why doancha take a walk down tha paper shop in the village an' get us a paper? Ceptin' he woulda pointed out we doan take a paper, and then he woulda pointed out it's gonna take him best part uvan hour there an' back, an' by the time he dun all that I'd be long finished in tha bedroom, and then tha lights are gonna come on an' he's gonna woyk out I'se only tryin'a get 'im outta my hair, an' that's gonna hoyt 'is feelins, which I ain't predisposed ta do.

So he brightens up, and takes the duvet in his two hands an' gives the cover a little tug. I says, Kowalski, it ain't gonna come clear like that. So he makes a face like he's tryina tear up a couple phone books, an' rips the duvet apart. They's buttons flyin' everywhere. I says, Kowalski, whaddaya playin' at?

He says, Mildred, I thought they was poppers.

Kowalski DIY

So. I got that Kowalski puttin' up some shelves. He's got the foldin' ladder. He's got the tool box'. He's got the power drill. He's got the head torch. I doan know why he's got the head torch. It ain't dark. He's got the power screwdriver. He says, Mildred, I needs a long screw.

Well, I hadn't got the heart, but I appreciated the opportunity. I says, I'll see whaddeye can do, dear.

He says, it ain't gowin' in straight. I goes to look fer the box a screws. I ain't sure how much more a this I can resist.

He shouts after me, I knows what ya thinkin', Mildred. I says, ya do, huh? He says, a course I do. He says, ya thinkin' this is gonna be a whole lot better than payin' ta get a man in.

I'm tellin' ya honey, that was the last thing I wus thinkin'.

Kowalski & A Christmas Tradition

Well, we were doing the Christams cards, that Kowalski and me. I always keep the ones we get each year, so we know who to send them to the next. Then he picks one out of order, off'n the pile. He says, who's Tom and Maureen?

I says, I doan know, dear. Which Tom and Maureen?

He says, what the hell sorta question is that? He says, how the hell many are there? He says, this Tom and Maureen, an' waves the card at me.

I says, Kowalski, lemme have a look. He says, I ain't never hoyd a noe Tom an' Maureen. He says, are they wan ya Bridge Club friends?

I says, I doan think so, dear. I says, is there anythin' written on the card. He says, a course there's sumpin' written on tha card. He says, how the hell else am I gonna noe who it's from? He says, it says Happy Christmas, from Tom and Maureen , an' he passs it over.

I says, I know it says that dear. I says, but does it say anything else. I says, sometimes people puts a message on the back, or maybe their address. He says, they ain't put nuthin' on the back a this wan Mildred, and I gotta admit, he's right.

I says, Kowalski, we must noe 'em from somewhere. I says, Kowalski, they bin sendin' Christmas cards fer years. Well that sure shuts him up, but not fer long.

He says, Milded, da you remember last Christmas? I says,

Kowalski, a course I remembers last Christmas. D'ya think I'm gowin' senile? He says, Mildred, a course I doan think ya gowin' senile. He says, but do ya remember last Christmas dinner? I says, a course I remembers last Christmas dinner. I says, we had Joe and Sharon over. He says, da you remember, when you was hangin' onta the bread sauce? I says, Kowalski I never hangs on ta the bread sauce. I says, Kowalski, I doan even like the bread sauce. I says, Kowalski, I only done made the bread sauce cos you likes it. He says, well you were takin' your time a passin' it around. Well, that sure shuts me up.

He says, but that ain't it. I says, it ain't? He says, a course it ain't. Sometimes ya gotta keep an open mind what Kowalski's gowin' on about. He says, you was hangin' onta it, on accounta what Sharon was tellin' ya. I says, I was? He says, sure ya was. I says, what wus she tellin' me? He says, she was tellin' ya they done got a Christmas card from two guys called Maurice and Julian. I says, she was? He says, a course she was. I says, well, that's very nice dear.

He says, Mildred, it ain't the very nice that's the point a it. I says, it ain't? He says, a course it ain't. He says, Mildred, she was tellin' ya they ain't got no gay friends, on accounta Joe bein' homyphobic. She was tellin' ya, they dint noe who this Maurice an' Julian was. I says, she was? He says, Mildred, a course she was. I says, but Kowalski, if they dint noe these two guys, how they noe they wus gay?

He says, Mildred, ya got the knack a gowin' straight ta the

heart a ya irrelevancy. I says, I do? He says, sure ya do. He says, it ain't the point whether or not the two guys a gay. He says, ya point a the story is they dint noe who sent 'em the card. I says, I dint noe no-one sent Maurice an' Julian a card. He says, no, no, no Mildred. It ain't the cards what got sent ta Maurice an' Julian, it's the card what they sent ta Joe an' Sharon. I says, it is? He says, a course it is. He says, doan ya see whaddit it means, Mildred? I says, no dear, I doan think I do.

He says, Mildred, it means we ain't the only wans getting' cards of'n complete strangers. I says, I suppose it does, Kowalski. He says, sure it does. He says, Mildred, they's gotta be a explination ta this. I says, there does? He says, sure they does. He says, an' Mildred, I thinks I done woyked out what it is. I says, Kowalski, tell me about it.

He says, we bin livin' a long time over here. I says, Kowalski, it sure feels that way sometimes. He says, Mildred, we done learned ta live the way the Romans is livin', metaphorically speakin'. I says, Kowalski, we sure have. He says, we eats the way they eats. He says, we drinks the way drinks, almost. He says, we dresses the way they dresses. He says, an' come ta talkin' we sounds like a couple a regular locals. I says, Kowalski, ya sure said a mouthful. He says, ain't it! He says, the only thing we's overlookin' is them local traditions ya doan even talk about, cozen ya takes 'em so much fer granted. I says, we do? He says, Mildred, I thinks maybe we do. I says, well, Kowalski, maybe ya's gotta point. I says, but what the hell.. I says, but what, dear, has that got ta do with the Christmas cards?

He says, Mildred, it's as plain as the nose on ya face, they got a tradition in this here place, a sendin' Christmas cards ta people they doan know. I says, they do? He says, a course they do. He says, that's why we's getting the card of'n Tom an' Maureen, and why theys getting' the card off'n ya Maurice an' Julian.

Well, whaddya gonna say ta that? I says, Kowalski, ya really think so? He says, Mildred, they ain't any other rational explanation. Then he pushes himself up off'n the table and goes out ta the hall. I says, whatcha dowin' dear? He says, I'm gonna get the phone book. I says, whaddya wan the phone book for? He says, I gonna write a Christmas card.

Well, he comes back in with the phone book an' slams it down on the table. He closes his eyes, and flips it open a coupla pages. He says, I'se gonna pick a name outta the fronta the phone book, an' he stabs his finger on it. He says, Mildred, who do I got? So I looks under his digit. I says, ya got Mr & Mrs T. Wilson-Smyth. He says, who? I says, Mr & Mrs T. Wilson-Smyth. He says, what the hell are they doin' at the fronta the phone book? I says, they ain't at the front. I says, Kowalski, ya done gottit upside down.

Ok, he says, Well, they's gonna have ta do. Then he takes wanna the expensive Christmas cards, that I keeps fer the closest friends. He says, I'm gonna send 'em this. He says, Mildred, this may be the last step towards our total integration inta this here society, an he writes Happy Christmas from Mildred and Me, on the card, an' he sticks it in the envelope, an' copies they's name an' address outta the phone book.

But I got little bells ringin' in the back a my head, now they's a sudden silence fallen while he's scribblin'.

He says, Mildred, I doan noe why we dint think a this before. He says, this is the natral way ya Enlishman's gonna take ta spread around a little Christmas cheer. It's cheap. It's friendly. It's anonymous, well, leastaways, it is as regards them bein' able ta track ya down an' bother ya, but ya gets ya name on the card, so ya sorta gets known fer ya good woyks. It's the poyfect blend a ya social an' ya private.

I says, Kowalski, I jes remembered who Tom an' Maureen are. I says, we met 'em on holiday, about three years back. That's when the cards started comin'. I says, we swapped addresses. I says, you wrote theirs in ya notebook. He says, which notebook? I says, the wan ya wus usin' around that time.
Then he tears up the expensive Christmas card he jus writ. I says, whatcha doin'? He says, we ain't good enough ta get a card of'n a stranger, the Wilson-Smyths kin go whistle for it. I says, what about the tradition? He says, what tradition? He's says, that Maurice an' Julian, why they's probably just a pair senile old men.

Kowalski & A Birthday Present

So I says ta that Kowalski, whatcha wan f'ya boythday?

He says, I doan know, Mildred. He says, I got mosta what I need.

I says, Kowalski, reason not tha need, that's Shakespeare ya know, I bin dooin' evenin' classes. I says, why doancha think a sumpin special, that ya gonna like a lot.

Then his face lights up, like a little boy's, the way they do, ya know! Well, I guess ya knows what's comin' next, an' I'm thinkin', well, even he does, I guess I will, seein' as it's his boythday, but I mean, I already got lots, an' ya can only wear wan at a time, well, unless, but at our age, ya doan wanna go makin' things more difficult than they are already.

But that ain't whaddee asks for. He says, Mildred, I'd like a Mandolin. I says, you'd like a mandolin, dear? He says, yeah. Mildred. I'd like a mandolin. That's whaddeyed like.

Well, that sure shuts me up. I'm thinkin' what put that idea inta his head. I mean, I know he likes ta help out in the kitchen, but a mandolin? That ain't ya regular piece a equipment. I mean, I dint even know he knew about slicin' ya vegetables that way. Then I remembers, the meal we has out, last week. We was with Joe and Sharon They was ya potatas, sliced that way, in ya cream. Sharon was sayin' howda they get tha potatas so thin. I says, they slice 'em with a mandolin. Then Kowalski, who I dint think was listenin' ta us, he says, these potatas are good, Mildred. He says, we oughta do our potatas like this sometime. Well, I thinks, if that's what'n he wants, that's whaddam gonna give him. But the other would a bin nice too, well, maybe I'll get 'im two presents, I mean ya doan know how many ya got left ta buy, do ya?

Well, I gets that little mandolin, from the cookery shop. It ain't much uva present ta my way a thinkin', but that Kowalski, he's always takin' ya by surprise. But I thinks, am gonna put it in a big box, so he woan know whaddit is till'n he gets it open. So I gets this box off'uv Sharon. She done jus' bought some fancy fryin' pan or other, an' that's whaddit came in. I thinks, he ain't gonna have any idea whaddeye got 'im.

So I wraps it up good an' proper, an' I puts on a little card. Ya shoulda seen his face. He ain't gonna have a clue, leastaways, that's whadd I'm thinkin'.

He says, Mildred, ya done, got it!

I says, I done got what?

He says, ya done got me a mandolin. Then he gives a big wet wan, on the cheek. He says, ya a princess, Mildred. He says, no ya not, yarra queen. Then he gives me another smacker. He says, more'n that Mildred, ya the Empress a the Universe, an' he starts tearin' off the wrapper.

I'm askin' ya, how the hell did he know, there was an itty bitty little mandolin, under all that wrappin'?

Kowalski & A House Spider

That Kowalski. He used ta tell this joke, about the diff'rence between a etymologist and a entomologist. I says, Kowalski, I doan even know what no entymologist is. He says, Mildred, that's tha point a the joke, and then he tells ya, ya etymologist is the wan what knows the diff'rence. Ya see, ya etymologist is man who knows about woyds. Well, then ya just gotta ask, ain't ya? I says, so what's an entomologist, dear? He says, a entomologist is a guy what studies ya insects. He says, ya thought ya got me there, Mildred, din't ya. I says, Kowalski, I would never a dreamed ya din't know.

So, it comes ta the day I'm gonna wash this big hairy spider down the plughole a the bath. He says, Mildred, ya cain't do that. I says, why not, dear. He says, ya gonna drown it. I says, Kowalski, I gonna wash it away. I says, I doan wan no spider in the bath. I says, ya spider comes crawlin' in my bath, it's gotta take its chances. So he says, here, let me get it, an he pulls out his hanky, and picks the great ugly beast up. So I opens the winder. He says, whatcha dooin'. I says I'm openin' the winder dear, so ya can throw it out.

He says, what the hell would I wanna do that for, Mildred? I says, so we can get rid of it, dear. He says, you gonna throw this baby outta the winder ya might'as well a washed it down the drain.

I says, Kowalski, whaddya talkin' about? He says, Mildred, this is a house spider. He says, how the hell else is it gonna get in ta the bath? He says, this spider ain't got no idea how ta get by you throw it outta the winder inta the big wide woyld. I says, whaddya mean it ain't got no idea a how ta get by? He says, Mildred, this spider has evolved ta go foragin' in ya floorboards an' under ya stairs. He says, it ain't got no way a dealin' with ya wilderness. He says, you throw this baby outta the winder, ya throwin' it ta tha wolves. I says, so Kowalski, whaddya gonna do with it? He says, Mildred, I gonna find it a nice quiet corner a the house, where it can get on with whaddits dooin' without you throwin' wan a ya wobblies cos it's in ya bath. And that's what he does.

So, a coupla weeks later we're at a social event an' the guy I'm sittin next ta tells me he's an entomolgist. He says, I guess ya doan know what that means, honey. Well, I tells him, apart from the fact that I ain't his honey, which I keeps ta myself, the way I hoyd it an entomologist is a guy what knows a lot more about insects than he does about women. Well, that sure shuts him up. Then I tells him about the house spider, and he starts fallin' about all over the place. He says, lady, ya kiddin' me. I says, no, you ask that Kowalski. He says, boy o' boy, I just gotta tell the guys back at the lab about this one. He says, lady they bin spiders livin' on this planet since before we even got down offa the trees. I says, you mean they ain't no house spiders after all? He says, a course they ain't. He says, they ain't got no idea whether they's in a mansion or in a mangrove swamp, 'ceptin' a course they'd be wetter in the swamp.

So ya see, it jus goes ta show. Ya might know the diff'rence between a etymologist an' a entomologist, but it sure doan make ya no entomologist.

Kowalski and a Name Badge

Let me tell you about the time we went shoppin' down the mall. I'm always tellin' that Kowalski, you wanna get people on your side you gotta call 'em by their names. It no use you sayin' hey boy, or excuse me miss, or say fella. He says, Mildred, how can I call 'em by their names, if'n I doan know what they names is? I says, well, dear, it ain't that difficult ta find out. He says, Mildred, how the hell I gonna find out what they names is? I ain't no detective, ya know.

I says, nobody's askin' ya ta be a detective, dear. All you gotta do is ask 'em. Then he gives me that little boy lost look. It's cute ain't it, but it ain't as cute as it used ta be. He says, Mildred, I doan like askin 'em. He says, what if'n they thinks I'm getting' fresh. I says, Kowalski, if they thinks ya getting' fresh ya takes their white stick off 'em an ya beats 'em with it.

He says, now ya makin' fun a me. I says, you knows I never made fun a ya in all my life, not even when we was doin' it with the noys's uniform. Well, that brings tha color ta his cheeks, ya know what I mean? I says, ya doan wanna ask 'em, ya just reads the little name badge they's wearin'.

So, we's in the ladies department, an' I'm lookin' through the racks. I needs a noo blouse, for when we got the Bridge Club comin' around next week. Then I hears a slappin' sound, an' it seems ta me it's the sorta slappin' sound ya gets when ya's slappin a Kowalski around. So I goes lookin', an' there he is. He's standin' next ta the ladies lingerie counter, lookin' red in the face, an' this itty bitty sales assistant lookin' like she done a good thing.

I says, excuse me honey, are you messin' with my man? She says, what, this old pervert? Well, I'm thinkin' maybe this is a time ta give her the weight a my handbag. We done just got a noo bottle a gin in there that mornin', but I can see she's bin brung up in a unimaginative household, so I gives her the benefit a the doubt. What's that honey? Well, I can see she wearin' a name badge says Kylie, on her left breast.

I says, what's goin' down Kowalski?

He says, I was just tryin' ascertain her name, Mildred. I says, sure you were, dear. Now you go on out ta the car park and wait for me there. Then I squares up ta little miss fisticuffs.

She says, that ole granddad, granddad, I ask ya, that ole granddad was lookin' at my tits.

I says, honey, he may a bin lookin' for ya tits, but he coytenly waren't lookin' at 'em. He done left his magnifyin' glasses at home.

Kowalski The Baby Sitter

Well, the neighbours are gowin' out for the night, but I'm at the Bridge Club, so that Kowalski, he gotta do the babysitting. I mean whatcha gotta do? The baby's bin fed. The baby's bin changed. The baby's bin read to. The baby's bin tucked up in its cradle. The cradle's bin rocked. The baby's bin sent ta sleep. They's only gonna be out a coupla hours. Anybody else'd have a sleepin' baby on their hands, the next four hours.

But not that Kowalski. Soon as they go out the door the baby's wakes up. As soon as the baby wakes up, it starts cryin'. Now that Kowalski knows about babies. He done brung up a couple a his own. So he rocks the cradle, but the baby keeps on cryin'. So he gives it a song, but the baby keeps on cryin'. So he reads it a story, but the baby keeps on cryin'. So he picks the baby outta the cradle and gives it a hug. The baby keeps on cryin'.

He says, Mildred, I's beginnin' ta wonder what's wrong. I says, what did ya do next, dear? He says, well, I thought it might be too hot, so I toyned down the central heatin', and opened the winda. He says, the baby went on cryin'. He says, Mildred, I thought maybe the baby was too cold, so I toyned up the central heatin' and shut the winda. He says, Mildred, the baby went on cryin'.

I says, you must bin getting' a little worried, dear. He says, Mildred, I wus sick with worry. He says, so I went round ta the neighbours.

I says, we are the neighbours, dear. He says, I went round ta Sharon and Joe's. They's the neighbours on the other side. He says, I says ta Sharon, will you come and look at the baby. So she come and look.

I asks him, What did she say, dear?

He says, Mildred, she says, this baby ain't too hot. It ain't too cold. She says, you checked its diapers? I says, I cain't smell nothin'. She says, neither can I. She says, this diaper a Terry? I says, a Terry? I says, I dint know diapers had names. I says, we had our kids a while back. She says, is it a terry towellin' diaper, or is it wan with a Velcro? She says, if'n it's a terry it might a got a safety pin come loose. So we has a look, an' it ain't, but the baby keeps on cryin'.

He says, Mildred, I asks her, what's wrong with it. She says, ain't nothin' wrong with it, 'ceptin' it ain't 'appy.

He says, Mildred, I was fresh outta ideas, an' it kept on cryin' right up until about five minutes before they gets back.

I says, Kowalski, dint they leave ya a bottle, dear?

He says, Mildred, sure, they left me a bottle, but I dint get time ta drink it.

5 EIGHT FRAMES FOR ROSIE WREAY

I

Rosie Wreay in the old folk's home. She is seated in her usual high-backed chair, at the far end of the room from the television, which has a large enough screen to be viewed comfortably from the street, and has the sound turned up loud enough to drown out any conversations within the room. She is slightly overweight, though she eats like a bird. But she gets no exercise these days, has gone beyond even the effort of taking a walk around the garden, where grey squirrels scamper across the lawns and run lightly along the tops of the wooden fences and leap to and from the rough trunks of the nearby pine trees. The autumn sun is strong in the garden. Rosie has aged. There are ninety-year-olds in the home who are more sprightly than she, but Rosie has barely turned eighty.

There's somebody to see you, Rosie, the Care Assistant says, touching her gently on the shoulder. Rosie looks up with a questioning expression on her face. The Care Assistant glances at Steven, and then adds, it's Randall...your son.

Rosie looks confused. She turns away from the Care Assistant to look at Steven. She stares at him, her mouth slightly open. He goes down on his haunches and smiles. It is a questioning smile. The two of them look at each other without speaking and the Care Assistant steps back, but does not leave. She looks down at Steven. She can see the resemblance between their two facing faces, but Steven, who is young-looking for his age, seems to her too old to be Rosie's son. He is more the age of a younger brother, she thinks, besides, there is no mention of a son in Rosie's file. There is no mention of any children.

Randall, she says, and Steven reaches out a tentative hand towards her.

Rosie's eyes narrow. She does not reach to meet his hand but leans slightly forward. Randall, she says, almost in a whisper, and then repeats it just as quietly. She settles back in her chair and closes her eyes. Randall, she says for a fourth time.

I don't think she recognises you, the Care Assistant says. She cannot understand it. Rosie does not have dementia. It is her physical health that they worry about. He must have moved away, she thinks, a long time ago, or maybe...the thought strikes her that it might be a case of mistaken identity, or that he is an imposter, but, seeing the two of them, face to face, she cannot deny the resemblance.

Steven, whose knees are beginning to ache, rises slowly to his feet.

No, he says, perhaps not.

II

The ruffles of nylon and lace on her nightie threw hazy shadows across her breasts. They moved like lightly touching fingers driven by the pulsing flames of the open fire. She was leaning against the half-open door of the darkened room.

He was taller than her, besides he was standing upright. He could see down into her cleavage. He could see the slightly darker circle of the aureole around her nipple through the thin, pink fabric. Her face was shadowed by the curls of her dark hair, and her eyes were darkened, by shadow and heavy blue makeup. Her voice was slurred. Come back in and have another drink, she said.

The man in the off-licence wrapped the bottle in pale tissue paper and slipped it inside a plastic bag. The boy pulled out a cheque already filled in.

I'm just collecting it for someone, he said. The shopkeeper took the cheque and read it. He looked up into the boy's face. The falling snow, which had settled on the shoulders of the boy's coat had melted to dark circles.

For the lady on the hill, the shopkeeper said, and smiled broadly. She'd be old enough to be his mother. She'd be in her mid-fifties. Twice his age, as usual, the shopkeeper guessed.

Is that what they call her? the boy wondered, and he realised that it was not the first time the shopkeeper had seen cheques written in that shaky hand, with that scrawled signature.

She's put the bank-card number on the back, he said. The shopkeeper didn't turn the cheque over, but put it into the till drawer.

That's fine, he said. He passed the plastic bag across the counter.

On the bed, on all fours above him, Rosie Wreay lifted her head from his erect penis and said, I only do this when I love. He didn't believe it, and as she resumed, he sat watching as her mass of dark hair rose and fell with the slow regularity of a pump-head.

III

It was some hell of a party I can tell you.

They used to have parties all the time. There was a lot of heavy drinking went on in that house. When I look back on it, well. They had Rasser living with them at the time. He was a big mate of Terry's in those days. There was a sofa bed in the corner of the room. It was a big flat. They'd invited Rosie Wreay. Do you remember her? She was OK. She was a good looker, but a bit on the thin side. She was divorced, I think. Of course, she and Rasser hit it off immediately. He'd be about five years younger than her, just turned thirty. They spent all evening talking to each other. There was some smoochie dancing, but mostly they just sat on that sofa bed and talked. I don't know what about.
The rest of us were talking politics. You know what it was like in those days. There was a strike every ten minutes, and the price of bread and potatoes was a weekly drama series. But Rosie and Rasser, it sounds like a double act, they were just head to head in deep conversation. Come about one in the morning the party fizzled out so I went home, but Terry told me the story a couple of days later.
Rosie was too drunk to drive, so she said she'd bed down on the carpet. Jill found her a sleeping bag. Rasser, being the gentleman he was, had failed to offer her the comfort of his sofa-bed, with or without incumbent. Talk they might have done, but apparently there was no spark so far as Rasser was concerned, besides, you

know what he was like. He'd probably had a couple of bottles of wine all to himself.

So they all bedded down. Terry and Jill had a little bedroom just off the main room. I don't know whether they heard what happened, or if Rasser told them about it the next day. Anyway, about the middle of the night, whenever that was, Rasser woke up with cramp in his leg. It was gloomy, rather than pitch dark. Maybe there was a moon shining in, I don't know. But the point was, Rosie, who wasn't sleeping all that well, could see the shape of Rasser's knee sticking up under the blankets like a tent pole, and she, so the story goes, misinterpreted it.

She must have thought Christmas had come, the size of it, and she called out, are you OK? Is there anything I can do for you? And Rasser, who was massaging his leg under the covers, said, I've got cramp, which she took to be a euphemism. So she was out of bed, and she leapt onto the sofa bed, only to find he had got cramp, and the tent pole was his leg. I don't think Rosie's of a particularly matronly turn of mind. Anyway, she wasn't interested in massaging his leg, and he wasn't interested in her massaging anything else, which, I know, might sound a bit strange where Rasser's concerned, but that was the way it was.

So she ended up being pissed off, and going home anyway. I think she told a similar story to Jill a couple of days later, but I only ever got Terry's version. I wish she'd spent the evening talking to me, I would have got cramp right where she needed it, let me tell you!

IV

You'd been out for a drink, after work.

You would sometimes do that. You lived in the city centre, and she lived up on the northern edge, where it peters out into marshy pastures and stands of pine trees up on the estuary. She was living in a squat in some old farmhouse where they were growing cannabis in the barn.

Some days she'd come in with eyes like pitted olives. You had a tiny office at the top of one of the big old terraced houses near to the bus station. A garret window looked out over rooftops and a brick built chimney stack that looked as if it were about to fall. A union man had his office downstairs, and someone from the Education Department, whom you never saw, on the middle floor. You had one funny shaped room, with a desk each, just out of sight of each other around a fold in the roof, and there was a sort anteroom opening onto the stairwell, where people could sit if they were waiting to be interviewed, and in which there was a sink and kettle. There was a toilet at the other side of the stairhead.

She was your secretary, but you could type as fast as she could, although not with your eyes closed. She used to dress in jeans and a man's shirt, and, what with her slim build, and the hairstyles of the time – she'd had hers frizzed up Afro-style – she could have passed herself off as some sort of androgynous boy. She had one of those delicate faces, like David Bowie, that you could dress up almost anyway you wanted and it would be attractive.

You were kids really. She was on the run, you always thought, but you had no idea what from. You were only a couple of years older than her. She would have been in her early twenties. The sixties were just kicking off. She didn't have a boyfriend, but everyone was talking about free love. You went out for a meal one evening, with a couple of the admin people from the head office, and you picked her up at the farm. When she walked out of the door your jaw dropped.

She was in a dress, with high heels and stockings, and carrying a little bag. Jesus, you said, you look fab. And it was as if you'd smacked her in the mouth. She just turned around and went back inside.

Rosie, Rosie! You called through the letterbox and banged on the door.

Just wait, she shouted, and her voice sounded hoarse. Then a few minutes later she came out again, this time in the jeans and man's shirt, as usual. You knew better than to ask why.

But it was after that, she turned up at the office in a summer frock, and you went for a drink after work, and had several, and she said, why not let's go back to the office, and make a coffee?
Which you did. You made it, and when you carried the two mugs back through into the little odd-shaped room with the desks, she was standing in front of her desk holding the hem of her frock between the thumbs and fingers of her hands.

What do you think? She asked, and pulled the thin fabric up to expose herself, naked beneath. Then you fucked her on the office floor, and when you'd finished, she said, that's another scalp. Then she told you that you were an easy lay, which was useful to know, you realised, later.

V

It was Mrs Bury what spotted it. She cleaned for the Burys, you know, Rosie Wreay, every Saturday for the last two years. They were going to offer her a job in the warehouse, when she left school. Of course, that's out of the window now, up the spout.

She was reaching up to dust the valance above the dining room window. That's a lovely room. Have you been in? Jack and I were invited last Christmas, for mince pies and a glass of sherry. Well, Jack and Mr Bury had port, but I find port too heavy, don't you? Unless you put something in it, and I wasn't sure that was the done thing, not at the Bury's, so I said, a sherry, please, sweet. But anyway, there she was reaching up and Mrs Bury could see.

She said, Rosie, come down here a minute, and she got her down off the chair and had a proper look, and said, is everything all right, Rosie? Well, of course, Rosie said, yes, Mrs Bury. The poor girl didn't even know she was. She didn't know a thing. Well, that's what I thought! She knew something. She knew what to do! Well, that's nature isn't it, and no-one had told her any better. But she had no idea one thing leads to another. I said, to Mrs Bury, hadn't she ever seen the dogs at it? Or the cats for that matter? Where did she think things came from?

Anyway, Mrs Bury told me, she said to her, Rosie, have you been getting yourself into trouble? Well, Rosie said, no Mrs Bury. She thought Mrs Bury was missing some silver or something like that. She hadn't a clue. Mind you, Jean Wreay's not the full shilling if you ask me. You'd have thought she have spotted it, her own daughter. She always was a daft 'apeth. I was at school with her.

By then it was too late to do anything about it. She was six months gone. I know! That would have made her thirteen and a half when she fell. What sort of man's going to do that to a thirteen year old girl? Well may you ask.

It was Charlie Balham got his name on the birth certificate. He let them spell it wrong they say, so that no-one would put two and two together. Charlie Balham. He's not a bad lad, is he? I never heard he was. But she's hardly Mata Hari is she? They must have been up to something mind you, or he wouldn't have agreed to it. He was paying too, out of his wages. He was apprenticed to Joe Sholey, at the cooperage, not that he'd be getting much there. There was talk of them getting married, but she was far too young. So was he as far as I could see. No more brains than his dad had.

Anyway, they put it up for adoption. Mrs Bury arranged it. She's friendly with the Matron at St Andrews. Got it taken with an older couple, couldn't have their own. Respectable. Got their own business. Mr Bury will keep an eye on things. Feels responsible I suppose, what with her working for them when it happened. Not that they had anything to do with it, nothing like that. Decent people, the Burys. Know how to behave. He's big in the Masons.

VI

All is over! It is goot!

The young man in the worn green shorts and the frayed peaked cap grinned. He was grasping the handles of an upended wheel-barrow from which he had just tipped a load of sand. You smiled up at him, shielding your eyes from the bright sun with your hand.

Are you still a prisoner? You asked. The man's grin broadened.

No more prisoner. Displaced person.

What?

I am a person in the wrong place. That is all. Soon, I go home. And the grin died on his face for a moment. Unless, I stay here, build houses.

Come on Fritz! A red skinned man, also dressed in shorts, though his were khaki, called from the far side of the building site. Where's that bleeding barrer?

The young man shook his head, lowered the handles, reverse turned the barrow, and wheeled it away.

Nazi bastard, Tommy said.

What?

That's what you call 'em. Pee, oh double yous. Nazi bastards. That's what my dad says. Tommy was older than you. Older, taller. He was even smoking. He had made a thin, hand rolled cigarette with a paper and a pinch of tobacco he'd taken from his dad's tin. His dad had a little machine that you could put the paper in, and the tobacco, and it would make a cigarette almost as good as one out of a proper packet. But Tommy had rolled his cigarette just between his fingers. One of the de-mobbed men had shown him how.

I missed this one, Tommy said, meaning the war, but I won't miss the next. He stuck the unlit cigarette in his mouth, made a machine gun with his empty hands and sprayed the German and the red-skinned man, who was now re-filling the barrow with sand, with imaginary bullets. Eh-eh-eh-eh, he said, trying not to spit out the cigarette.

Tommy turned to you and grinned. You got 'em?

You gave him a knowing look.

Wouldn't you like to know. Tommy raised a hand.

None of your cheek. Well, have you?

I might have. But not here. You glanced across to the row of derelict houses. Tommy looked up too. They had no door or window frames, and someone had already begun to remove the blue slates from the roofs. Dusty light split by the barred shadows of the slateless laths showed through the upper windows. The lower floors, where the ceilings were still intact, were gloomy caves.

Come on then, he said. Excitement kindled his eyes. You tipped back your head and gave him a tight smile. You walked across the no-man's land between the building site and the bombed out terrace, slipped in through a chipped doorway. You stood in the middle of the floor.

What do you want 'em for? You asked.

Never you mind. He said, following you in. You noticed that his hand, which had reached up for the cigarette, was slightly trembling.

You knew anyway. You'd seen your brother do it.

Have you got 'em or not? His voice had gone lower, rougher, like gravel slithering over a corrugated sheet. You pursed your lips, then, putting a hand in your pocket pulled out something pale and stringy.

I got this, you said, in a silky voice. You let the suspender belt unravel and dangle from your hand, biting your lip. Tommy swallowed, and then made a grab for it. You didn't let go, and for a moment you stood, barely a pace apart, each holding one end of the strip of fabric. The metal hangers glinted in the gloom. Come on Rosie, he said. You let go. There's weren't any knickers, you said, not that you'd like.

You don't know what I'd like, Tommy said, stuffing the suspender belt in his pocket..

You smiled, and held out your hand.

We agreed, you said. He put his hand back in his pocket and pulled out a small bar of chocolate, placed it on your palm. You grinned and closed your fingers over it. And one of those, you said, nodding towards the cigarette, next time, when I bring the knickers.

You're too young, he said. You pulled a face, raising your

eyebrows and twisting your mouth into a lop-sided smile. All right, he said.

Let me see you light it, you said, stuffing the chocolate bar away.

I don't want it, at the moment, he said. You pulled the face again.

He pulled out a zippo and flamed it up, held it to the cigarette and inhaled. A fit of coughing racked him and his eyes watered. You reached out and took the cigarette from his mouth. You put it in your own and drew in a long breath. Closing your eyes and moving your closed mouth like someone savouring food, you blew out smoke through your nose.

Monday, you said, will be her next washing day. Then you passed him back the cigarette and walked back out into the sunlight. In the darkness inside you could hear him coughing.

VII

Jean Wreay had never liked thunder. With Billy away it was even worse.

They're a long way off, Hermione Bury, said, and she reached out a slender white hand and touched Jean's arm. They're after Rolls Royce, at Derby.

That's where they were aiming for when Edward Street got hit, Jean reminded herself. What if they hit the Bury's warehouse? All those cigarettes going up.

We'll be fine, Hermione Bury said, and she looked down at little Rosie, and said, won't we?

How did she do it, Jean wondered? Hermione's own boys were away, Charles still at school, the older brother in the navy somewhere, being bombed, torpedoed, God knew what. And Charles was likely to be called up they were saying.

Nobody blinked. She could see their eyes, in the flickering light of the little lamp. Derek Fitton had rigged it up for them, using a car battery. He'd made one for himself, before he'd gone away. Even little Rosie didn't blink, but just sat there, holding on to her mother and looking up into their faces. Little Billy, who was just like his dad, was curled up asleep at the back of the shelter. She could never tell what Rosie was thinking. Not since that afternoon, back in the spring. She would have to talk to her about that, before Billy came back. When she knew Billy was coming back. That would be when they'd need to talk about it. No use crossing bridges before you reach them.

She remembered Rosie's big unblinking eyes when she walked into the bedroom. The American boy had rolled off her, his thing still sticking up – he hadn't come off – and he'd said-- perhaps it was the drink had made him so unabashed, so unconcerned – hello, little lady, who are you?

When the all clear sounded, Rosie asked, can we go up now mummy?

VIII

Billy Wreay folds his arms and rocks back on his heels. There is a big grin on his face. He has painted up the old pram, which Hermione Bury has dug out of the stables at the back of the house. Take this Billy, it'll do up nicely. I shan't be wanting it again, and by the time Charles and his brother get round to having children they'll be using something quite different I expect. They'll have electric prams or heaven knows what.

Are you sure, Mrs Bury?

Yes, go on, take it. I don't why know why I ever kept it, but it's a good thing I did!

Billy has sanded it down, and cleaned it, and repaired one or two little cracks here and there, and done his best to straighten the spokes of the wheels so that they look almost right. And Jean has sewn some bedclothes from old blankets, and Derek Fitton, looking wistful, has given him the remains of the hood from a scrapped Austin. So, all in all, it looks a pretty good pram, and what with the dolly that Jean's sister had given Rosie, it has turned into a very successful third birthday party.

Rosie is bent over it, tucking little Randall – where she has got that name from he has no idea – tucking little Randall, into his new bed.

Of course it's a boy, dad, she says, putting her hands on her hips.

Wouldn't you prefer it to be a baby girl? Billy asks. The doll certainly looks, to his eyes, like a baby girl.

You have to take what you're given, dad, she says. That, she has picked up from her mother. But, he wants to say, it is a baby girl. Jean, who is standing behind Rosie, purses her lips and shakes her head.

Randall though? Who, in their family, would ever have a boy called Randall?

6 ANOMALIES
(THREE STORIES TO END ON)

Woy Dincha?

Oad that roap, he sed, annie throo me t'end uvit. Dunner let go, and oald ard or itull pull yer off yer feet. So ah grabbed roap an ung on. Ee were up tree wi chayne sore. Ee luckt dahn and sed ,Woy dincha?
Woy dinta woh?
Woy dincha givver wan?
It wern a marrera givvinner wan. It were a marrera rug orra kiss.
Well, woy dincha giver wan a them?
Ah sed, well, she myra corld rape.
Dunt be daft, he sed. She wannidit as much as yoo, if ah nose aht abaht wimmin.
Then ee pulled cord and chayne sore went off an ee set it tut branch. An branch cum wallopin dahn, twistin as it fell, an pulled me clean off mi feet, just loike ee sed it wud.

Which is exactly what I'd been afraid of when it came to the moment of kissing.

The Best He Could Do

I told him,

There was this writer, walked into a barber's shop in Penrith and said, Is there an O'Neill in here? And everyone in the place fell silent and turned to look, and a young barber stopped what he was doing and spun around with a cut throat razor covered in foam in his hand, and said, I'm an O'Neill, Who wants to know?

And the writer said, I do, because I'm going to tell you a story about an O'Neill. It took place about thirty years ago not more than twenty miles from here.

And the young barber wiped the scutter from the blade of the open razor and listened.

Then the writer said, I think the O'Neill's first name might have been Thomas, but it's a long time back, and he ran this barber's shop at the time, and the young barber said, That's my grandfather, and he took a pace forward, stropping the blade.

And then the writer said, It was at the hospital in Carlisle City, where the old man was waiting on his mother to die. She was a gypsy queen, he said, and the young barber said, So she was, and his eyes burned steady in his head.

Then the writer said, I was in the next room, alone, touched with an illness that put me in fear of death for a couple of years, and on account of needing to be isolated. But the door was left open, and the O'Neill looked in, passing on his way to take a break, and told me the tale of his mother and asked if there was anything he could do for me.

And the young barber stayed silent and still and listened.

Then the writer said, And the O'Neill came back from his break and brought in a packet of biscuits which he gave to me – chocolate digestives I think they were – and his mother I think died later that night or the one after, for I never laid eyes on him again. And that was an unexpected gift in a dark hour from one stranger to another before an uncertain dawn.

And all the men in the chairs and the barbers by their sides had stopped their talking and their cutting and shaving and were listening and watching. And the writer said, And I've come here today to bear witness to that act of kindness, and to show that it has never been forgotten and has always been honoured, though it's long overdue in the showing.

And the man I was telling asked, Is that a true story? And I said, well, some of it is. The giving and receiving took place, though the biscuits were different; but that writer, though he walked past the door of that barber-shop from time to time over the decades, and always meant to go in and pay his respects, never did so, but just wrote this story.

Babylon 38D

We met Joyce in the pub garden.

What do you think of the gardens? she asked.

It was a garden-club trip. We'd arrived in several cars and parked on the village green. A dozen gardens were open to the public for the day in aid of charity.

Did you see the bras? she asked, waiting until my wife had slipped off to the loo.

I'd seen them. In a garden by the old mill-race. A dozen different bras, different colours, different styles, different sizes, hanging from the pergola, done up like hanging baskets. In fact, I'd thought they were hanging baskets, until the woman whose garden it was sidled up to me and said, nice, aren't they? I realised what I was looking at, and blushed. They were all at eye level. If someone had been wearing them, you would have been on your knees before her.

They were supposed to be all over the village, she explained. It's a W.I. project. Then she frowned, and said, you're not a local?

Not born and bred, I said, which, I knew was what she meant.

She smiled. Some of the local men, she said, are a bit traditional, so all the bras ended up here. They were uncomfortable with having to look at them, in their own gardens. Their wives have donated them.

They're good aren't they? Joyce said, the bras.

I had to admit they were.

It certainly raises issues, I said. She nodded, encouragingly. I mean, are you supposed just to enjoy the flowers, or are you expected to get a buzz off the underwear? Or would that make you some sort of pervert?

Well, she said, whatever lights your candle! That's what they're designed for. And I'll swear her eyes flicked down towards my lap. I could feel my face tingling. Did any of them spark you up? She asked.

I might have glimmered a little, I said, at one or two. I crossed my legs.

She glanced towards the loos, then leaned in closer.

Did you....?

What?

She lifted both hands, palms up, fingers crooked.

Did you? Her hands rose and fell gently, heft any?

No!

She shook her head.

The woman, at the bra garden, had told my wife how you sewed up the backs to make the cups into pouches. Then you fill them with compost, she said, and she reached up and squeezed one purple, lace covered breast. She'd glanced at me then, and swung the bra towards me, for closer inspection.

It's crazy, I said to Joyce, with everything we see these days, in the papers and on TV - she smiled encouragingly - how potent – I couldn't think of a better word – those bras, were, you know, I mean, in the candle lighting department.

Her smile grew wider.

That's because you were so close, she said, and knew they'd had real women inside them.

Then my wife re-appeared and asked, what are you two talking about? And I said, about the gardens.

ABOUT THE AUTHOR

Brindley Hallam Dennis has published several collections of short stories and a novella. His work has been widely performed and published in magazines, journals and anthologies. Writing as Mike Smith he has published poetry, short plays and essays. His plays are available through Lazy Bee Scripts. He regularly writes for Thresholds, the International Post Graduate Short Story Forum. He lives in north Cumbria within sight of three mountain tops and a sliver of Solway Firth. He blogs at www.Bhdandme.wordpress.com

Second Time Around (short stories)
A Penny Spitfire (novella)
Talking To Owls (short stories)
Departures (short stories)
Ambiguous Encounters (short stories with Marilyn Messenger)
Ten Murderous Tales (short stories)
The Man Who Found A Barrel Full of Beer (short stories)

As Mike Smith
The Broken Mirror (poetry)
No Easy Place (poetry)
Valanga (poetry)
Martin? Extinct? (poetry)
English of the English (essays on A.E.Coppard)
Readings for Writers vol.1
The Poetic Image (a short course in the short story)
Love and Nothing Else (Readings for Writers vol.2)
The Silent Life Within (Readings for Writers vol.3)
An Early Frost (poetry)

Made in the USA
Charleston, SC
03 November 2016